# THE PHONY MARINE

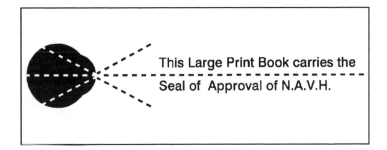

This Large Print Book carries the
Seal of Approval of N.A.V.H.

# THE PHONY MARINE

## JIM LEHRER

**THORNDIKE PRESS**

*An imprint of Thomson Gale, a part of The Thomson Corporation*

**THOMSON**

━━━✶━━━ ™

**GALE**

Detroit • New York • San Francisco • New Haven, Conn. • Waterville, Maine • London

# THOMSON
# GALE
™

Thorndike Press® Large Print Basic.

The text of this Large Print edition is unabridged.

Other aspects of the book may vary from the original edition.

Set in 16 pt. Plantin.

**LIBRARY OF CONGRESS CATALOGING-IN-PUBLICATION DATA**

Lehrer, James.
   The phony marine / by Jim Lehrer.
     p. cm.
   ISBN-13: 978-0-7862-9338-4 (lg. print : alk. paper)
   ISBN-10: 0-7862-9338-1 (lg. print : alk. paper)
   1. Impersonation — Fiction. 2. Marines — Fiction. 3. Large type books.
  I. Title.
PS3562.E4419P48 2007b
813'.54—dc22                                   2006037577

Published in 2007 by arrangement with Random House, Inc.

Printed in the United States of America on permanent paper

10 9 8 7 6 5 4 3 2 1

*LEHRER*

*JIM*

For the real marines —
particularly my late father,
Fred Lehrer, Sr.,
and my brother, Fred Lehrer, Jr.

Now, you guys have had a
nice, easy day.
I hope you enjoyed it, because
it's the last one
you're gonna get for a long time.
You joined the marines.

— JOHN WAYNE
as Sergeant John Stryker
in *Sands of Iwo Jima*

# ONE

Hugo Marder returned to his Dupont Circle town house to find two small packages among the normal clutter of mail. There was also a D.C. superior court jury summons.

Both of the boxes were book-size "Fly Like an Eagle" Priority Mail boxes from the U.S. Postal Service. He knew they were eBay auction purchases.

The return address on one signaled that a pair of cuff links were inside that featured a plastic-enclosed miniature black-and-white photo of Mike Nichols on one, Elaine May on the other. Hugo had paid fifty-one dollars, plus five dollars for shipping and insurance. He had truly loved Nichols and May's humor when he was in college in the sixties, but it was their pictures on cuff links that interested him now. Hugo was a collector of antique and unusual cuff links, a hobby that had sprung naturally out of his early interest in graphics and, now, from his work at Nash Brothers, America's leading merchant of quality men's clothes.

It was the other package that really interested him. He knew what was in it, too, because it came from "J. Wayne, 134 West Mistletoe, San Diego, California."

He first took a hard look at the jury notice and, after noting the summons date to be four weeks away, carried it with the San Diego box to his desk in the den. He wrote the court day in his calendar and clipped the printed notice to the page. He knew the district's juror drill, having been called three times to serve.

Then he picked up the package.

His hands shook slightly as he ripped back the box lid. He was not usually a person who quivered and shook with emotional anticipation — not on birthdays or Christmas mornings as a kid, or even before marrying *or* divorcing Emily.

He retrieved a clump of bubble wrap. The case was down there inside the bubbles. He could see it.

The wrap came off easily, and suddenly he was holding the case in his two hands.

It resembled a jewelry box, about seven inches long, three and a half or so wide, maybe an inch thick. As the auction description had said, the case was covered in imitation black leather with two wavy gold-leaf lines around the edge, a half inch apart, creating a frame effect. In the center, also in gold, were the words SILVER STAR MEDAL.

"Silver Star medal," he read out loud. And then, as if making an announcement on a train station PA, he said again, "Silver Star medal."

Here was a Silver Star medal. He was holding a case with a Silver Star medal inside.

Hugo lifted the lid, which was lined in off-white silk.

There was a tiny metal lapel button.

A small rectangle ribbon for regular uniform use.

And then the real medal — the pendant and full ribbon.

The auction listing had said only that the lapel pin appeared to have never been taken out of its case and that all three items were in excellent condition. That had certainly turned out to be true.

They were mounted on a bed of peach-colored felt. They were perfect.

Hugo touched the pendant, which was hanging from a piece of red, white, and blue ribbon. It was a five-pointed gold star, an inch and a half in diameter, with a laurel wreath in the middle and a quarter-inch-size silver star in the center of the wreath.

He turned it over. On the back was engraved: FOR GALLANTRY IN ACTION. Below that, in slanted type: *Ronald Derby Cunningham.*

Hugo slipped the medal out and held the whole thing in his right palm. The eBay listing had said Cunningham performed his act of heroism while serving as a U.S. Marine lieutenant in the Vietnam War, but there were no specifics about what he had done.

Hugo also had no idea what route this exquisite piece of ribbon and metal had taken from Cunningham to him.

He wondered seriously now, as he had only slightly before, why anybody would be selling Cunningham's — or anybody else's — Silver Star? Hugo had no military experience, having avoided service during the Vietnam War. It was a fact of his early life's experience that he had, somewhat to his surprise, grown increasingly and obsessively to regret. The drive of U.S. troops toward Baghdad right now had served to heighten that feeling.

Abruptly, he regretted possessing this medal of another man's heroism. There was something not right about auctioning off or buying a medal that Ronald Derby Cunningham, whoever he was, had surely risked his life to win.

Hugo comforted himself with the thought that he had bought this Silver Star on eBay impulse, almost by accident.

He set the medal down on the desk and lifted the smaller uniform ribbon and the even smaller lapel pin out of the case. The pin was a tiny — five eighths of an inch long, only an eighth wide — enameled replica of the red, white, and blue ribbon.

Hugo went to his computer, opened it to his deleted e-mail file, and fired off a message to jwayne@net.com. "I just received the Silver Star medal set — eBay item #52613835. I am interested in its history. Would you mind e-mailing me any details concerning how it came to be on the market, etc.? Thanks. Hugo Marder — goodsuit@aol.com."

And he waited, virtually motionless.

After thirty-five minutes with no response, he clicked on Google, the Internet search engine he used most often. In its Search box, he typed "San Diego." After a couple of beats, a list of directories and websites came up. He clicked on "City Directory" and typed "134 West Mistletoe." Soon came a name, "V. Heflin," and a phone number.

Hugo dialed the number.

Somebody with a hoarse male voice answered. He said there was no person by the name of V. Heflin at this number — or the Mistletoe Street address, when Hugo followed up — and there never had been.

"You must be Mr. Wayne, then, right?"

"He died," said the man.

Hugo expressed sympathy and asked if somebody there, by any name, had sold a Silver Star medal via eBay to a Hugo Marder in Washington, D.C.

"Nope," said the voice, the volume now down to near zero. "But if anybody did, it wouldn't be against the law. Everything except the Medal of Honor. Tradin' in 'em is illegal. But the Navy Cross on down, no problem. Iraq's causin' business to go up again. You a medal cop?"

Hugo said he was not a cop of any kind, and legality was not the problem — not the reason he was calling. "I just want to know out of simple curiosity how it came to be on the market," he said. "I bought it, and now I want to know what happened to Mr. Cunningham, the marine who won the medal, and how it came to be up for auction —"

Hugo heard the phone click dead at the other end. It was followed by the dial tone.

The nonconversation about Ronald Derby Cunningham's Silver Star was over.

Hugo figured the guy in San Diego, whoever he really was, had borrowed the names of John Wayne and Van Heflin, two of the most famous movie marines, for his eBay business. *The Washington Post* had run a story recently about people using phony names online, some to protect their privacy and others to pull fast ones.

Hugo's childhood dream had been to be a U.S. Marine. He had seen John Wayne as Sergeant Stryker in *Sands of Iwo Jima* and Van Heflin as Major Sam Huxley in *Battle Cry* several times.

Tomorrow. Tomorrow he would get on to doing something about this Silver Star. He would think about — and decide — what he might do to find out about the medal — *my* medal . . .

*My* medal? That was not a good and healthy thought. Even having considered such a thing now brought warmth to Hugo's face. This Silver Star would always belong to Ronald Derby Cunningham, whoever and wherever he was.

On the other hand. There it was. That medal lay right in front of Hugo, here on this desk. He had purchased it for eighty-five dollars plus postage and insurance from somebody in California with a phony name. As the guy had said, it was all perfectly legal.

Hugo picked up the little lapel button and stuck it in his buttonhole. He was wearing a charcoal-gray poplin two-button suit, the same one he had worn at work all day. He had been so anxious to open the package that he had failed to take off his coat, something he usually did the moment he walked in the house. Quality clothes needed and deserved quality care.

He went into the entrance hall. There was a narrow full-length mirror on one wall that he looked at automatically each morning as he left for the store. Nash Brothers insisted that its salesmen — sales associates, they were called officially — dress in Nash Brothers clothes, and that they wear those clothes well. "Could there be a better advertisement for our merchandise and our soul than that?" said the man who had trained Hugo.

The Silver Star lapel button looked good — natural, at ease — against the charcoal-gray background. Hugo chose to ignore the additional non-marine mirror image of a balding, slightly overweight man in his mid-fifties.

He decided to go for a walk and maybe get a sandwich from one of the take-out establishments in the neighborhood. He didn't have anything in the house to eat.

There was a new Greek place specializing in gyro sandwiches; it had opened only a few weeks ago. Hugo had been meaning to give it a try. Why not tonight? Why not take a stroll over to it right now and pick up a gyro?

What could be the harm in that?

Hugo's home on Nineteenth Street, Northwest, was a narrow three-story brick structure with a front door painted crimson red. The door had been red when he bought the place three years ago, and he had originally intended to paint it gray or beige — something more ordinary, more him. "More Hugo," in the annoying words of Emily, his runaway ex-wife. But the flash of the red, to his surprise, began to grow on him, and eventually he had repainted it an even brighter red. He was also probably making a statement — or, more coarsely, a form of shooting the finger — to Emily. She never would have thought of Hugo, the straight and dull clothing salesman, as somebody who would live behind a red door. Only people from her exciting, important world of Congress, the government, and war-and-peace, would do such a wild and crazy thing. Hugo had even considered using his cartooning skills to draw a giant grinning face in black on top of the red. That would have really gotten to Emily.

Now, with that red door closed behind him, Hugo walked in the early-evening crispness south to the corner and then west on R Street toward Connecticut Avenue. It was only a few minutes before six-thirty, and there was still some daylight left.

He passed no other pedestrians in the first block. But in the next block, here came a couple in their late twenties, fairly well dressed. Congressional aides, no doubt. Maybe interns, maybe think-tank assistants.

As they passed, Hugo made no eye contact with either of them, although it seemed to him that the young man glanced at his lapel button. But with no recognition. That figured. Nobody that kid's age would know about a Silver Star medal. The most recent wars, including the first with Iraq, had not aroused such interest. Maybe this second Iraq war would.

At Connecticut Avenue, he turned right, toward the new Greek place. Hugo figured this area around Dupont Circle had more places to eat per square inch than any comparable space in Washington, if not the civilized world. They ranged from fancy restaurants with high-class menus, chefs, and prices that served cabinet secretaries and media personalities, to cheap dives with blackboard menus, microwaves, and for-student prices that served from behind walk-up counters. Even in nearly six years in the neighborhood — including the time he rented — Hugo had barely scratched the surface of what was available.

He passed a Thai restaurant that was known as one of the best and most exotic in Washington. The large red, green, and yellow neon sign above the door announced the establishment's name as THE HOUSE ON THE KLONG. He was no big fan of Thai food, so he had never been inside. But he had read that it was supposedly patterned after a house in Bangkok that once belonged to Jim Thompson, the silk king. Hugo knew about Thompson. There was a high-quality line of Jim Thompson silk ties that were made especially for Nash Brothers, most featuring tiny elephants in various patterns and colors.

The sidewalks along Connecticut, as was true most evenings, were loaded with people. Again, the youngest ones paid no attention to the Silver Star button in his lapel, but a few of the older men did. A man who appeared to be in his early sixties actually nodded in a kind of Episcopal motion to the cross. Good for you, sir, thought Hugo.

He came to one of his favorite places, a French brasserie named after the Belgian writer Georges Simenon. Its specialties were heavy lentil-and-goose dishes and strong after-dinner liqueurs, particularly calvados, a brandy made from apples. Hugo had a large glass one night and paid for it dearly the next day with a hammering headache and nausea that would not go away. Thank God it had been a Sunday morning, so it didn't affect his performance on the floor at the store.

He was almost to the Washington Hilton, where John Hinkley shot Ronald Reagan and Jim Brady, and the gigantic statue of Union general George McClellan on horseback in full dress regalia. Hugo didn't know or care much about the Civil War, but he had a vague notion that Abraham Lincoln had considered McClellan a risk-averse jerk who should have won more battles than he did. But why, then, was there a statue of him in such a prominent place in Washington?

This was also where the restaurants and other shops ran out and apartments and embassies and embassy residences began.

Farther on was the William Howard Taft Bridge, which crossed high above Rock Creek and Rock Creek Parkway and was known mostly for the two huge lions sitting royally on their haunches on either side of the entrance. Through the years, several people, some of them reasonably prominent, had climbed over the bridge's chest-high metal railings and jumped to their death into the creek, the tall trees of the park, or the road two hundred feet below.

After crossing Connecticut by the Hilton, Hugo headed back south toward the Greek deli. The San Antonio Café was on the corner. The Tex-Mex place looked festive inside — men in suits, but with their shirt collars open, and women in very short skirts, most in large groups at large tables, laughing and smoking and drinking margaritas.

Hugo had never been part of any evening like that. Not even back in Michigan at Big Rapids, or at college in Kalamazoo, except the few times he'd had a beer with three or four other students who shared some interest in cartooning.

Here was Zorba's, his destination. It was clean, unpretentious, white and chrome, with a small section for in-house eating in addition to the take-out counter.

The menu was printed on a large black-and-white poster above the counter, with HOME OF THE GYRO written above. Hugo glanced at the other possibilities: kebab sandwich, taco Europe (ground meat and finely chopped vegetables baked on pita dough), spinach pie, falafel, and a variety of pizzas and salads.

The man behind the counter was in his forties, large, dark-skinned, black-haired. Was he Mr. Zorba? Was there a Mr. Zorba? Was Zorba a first or last name, or only that of the movie character played by Anthony Quinn?

"Can I help you?" the man asked Hugo in an accent that was pure Northeast American. His eyes went right to Hugo's coat lapel, to the Silver Star. His face broke out in a magnificent smile. His brown eyes sparkled. It was clear he was looking at somebody important, somebody impressive — somebody very special. It was a look, a response, that Hugo had never received from anyone.

"How about a chicken gyro?" Hugo said.

"Gyros are what got us here," the man said. "With some white yogurt sauce? That's a specialty, too."

"Sounds good," Hugo said.

A teenage girl who, by her appearance,

could have been the man's daughter went to work on the order.

"You win that Silver Star in Vietnam?" the man asked Hugo. His tone was that of a little boy asking Hank Greenberg how he'd hit that curveball out of the park.

On reflex, Hugo nodded.

"My uncle won the Bronze Star in World War Two. He went ashore at Anzio."

Hugo smiled.

"What happened? How did you win it?" the man asked.

Hugo shrugged modestly.

"Army?"

"Marines." The word just came out.

"Marines are the special ones. Look what they're doing in Iraq right now. Bet they beat the army to Baghdad. The Few. The Best. Isn't that what they say in the commercials?"

"Something like that," Hugo said. He knew exactly what they said on TV and on billboards and in the magazine ads about the marines needing a few good men.

"There's another marine around here. He came in a couple of weeks ago, right after we opened. He had one of those lapel things for the Navy Cross. That's even a bigger deal, isn't it? Second behind the Medal of Honor for you marines and navy guys? Not that a Silver Star isn't great."

Hugo felt a warmness rise up through his body to his face.

"He wears his hair short and walks straight up, like he's in a parade. But he seems a lot older. Probably World War Two, maybe Korea. I asked him, and he said something about a place I'd never heard of. He really didn't want to talk about it. Makes you wonder why he wears the thing on his coat, doesn't it? But what the hell, I'd wear it if I had it, no matter what. I think my uncle slept with his Bronze Star thing on his pajamas."

Hugo said nothing. And, in a few seconds, there was his sandwich, wrapped neatly in shiny silver foil. The man stuck it in a white paper sack and handed it over. The menu board said the price of a chicken gyro was four-fifty. Hugo laid a five-dollar bill on the counter.

The man pushed the money back his way. "This one's on the house — on me, Johnny Zorba."

"No, sir. I can't let you do that."

"You live around here?"

"Yes, over on Nineteenth Street."

"Next time, and all the next times after that, you pay. Not this time. You earned this gyro in Vietnam. I gave the Navy Cross guy a kebab. Marines matter to me — they should to everybody, particularly right now, when we're going after Saddam's nukes."

Hugo mumbled agreement and a thank-you, took the bag, shook Johnny Zorba's hand, and walked off.

Once outside and away from Zorba's, he reached up to remove Ronald Derby Cunningham's Silver Star lapel button from his charcoal-gray suit coat. He had just accepted a free sandwich under the falsest of false circumstances. He was a fraud, a liar — a thief.

But. As he ran his forefinger over the pin, the enamel felt smooth, slick, good — still very much at ease. He did not take it out of his lapel. Instead, he let his hand fall back down against his side.

He slowed his pace. There was no need to rush back to the house.

Before arriving back at the red door, Hugo Marder received two hero acknowledgments and nods of admiration for Ronald Derby Cunningham's Silver Star.

He was trying to race through water up to his chest and weeds up to his nose with his sketch pad in his right hand and a machine gun in his left. He was carrying both high over his head. He was in a dress marine uniform

25

with white pants, the creases perfect, and a hat and a red tunic like the kind the U.S. Marine band wore on television at the White House and when it gave concerts on the Capitol grounds and in parades down Pennsylvania Avenue. Under the red coat, he was wearing an oxford-cloth double-weave pink dress shirt with French cuffs. He could see Nichols and May cuff links sticking out and shining in the Vietnamese sunshine. He should have worn the ones with the presidential seal. He had a pair with the signature of Gerald Ford, our Michigan president, engraved on the back of each.

Bombs that smelled like Thai food were dropping on him and exploding. He heard cracks of what sounded like small-arms fire, and he felt stings in his right arm and then in both of his legs. He had been hit. Blood was flowing from his right arm and both legs but also from his nose and ears. He could see it on his white pants — what a cleaning job they would need! — but not on his red coat. Thank God it was red on red. He kept running.

"Move out, marines!" he screamed. "Kill the Japs, marines!"

He looked behind him. There was John Wayne. Van Heflin. And Johnny Zorba, running hard to stay up while tossing hot chicken gyros wrapped in aluminum foil at the gooks.

The gyros were exploding, tearing gooks who tried to catch them into chicken shreds. Zorba was wearing a charcoal-gray suit with a Navy Cross pinned to the knot of his tie, which was a Jim Thompson silk with yellow elephants on a bed of dark blue.

"You're my hero!" Zorba yelled. "Hero! Hero! If you can't do it, nobody can!"

"I'm not the hero, you're the hero!" Hugo yelled back.

"Gyro! We're the Home of the Gyro, not the hero!" Zorba screamed back.

Just behind Zorba was a beautiful young woman in a dress marine uniform, but her skirt was way too short — across her crotch. Hugo could see her thighs as she ran. There was no telling what he'd see if she crossed her legs as she sat down at a restaurant table. He recognized her face as that of the hostess at an Italian restaurant in the neighborhood. He hadn't known she was also a marine. She was knocking down Japs with the framed picture of a cathedral in Florence, Italy.

President Ford had personally asked him to take out this patrol. "Do it for Sergeant Stryker and Major Huxley and John Wayne and Van Heflin and for Emily and for America and for the Michigan Wolverines, Lieutenant Ronald Derby Cunningham." Hugo told him he would but that he was Hugo Marder of Nash Brothers, not Lieutenant Ronald Derby Cunningham of the marines. He said also that he had gone to Michigan Western State College in Kalamazoo, not the University of Michigan at Ann Arbor, and doing something for the Michigan Wolverines wasn't something that he saw as a particularly natural or heroic thing to do.

"Heroes do what comes naturally in every situation, Lieutenant Cunningham," said Mr. Ford. "And you are a hero."

"I am not a hero," Hugo said.

"I am the president, I will decide that," said Mr. Ford. He asked Hugo to step forward, and he stuck a Silver Star lapel button into a buttonhole on the front of his tunic. "For conspicuous gallantry and intrepidity in action, I present this to you, Lieutenant Ronald Derby Cunningham, for your actions, which reflected great credit upon yourself and upheld the highest traditions of the Marine Corps, the United States Naval Service, the Michigan Wolverines, and Zorba's, the Home of the Gyro."

Wayne and Heflin said together, "Well done, marine."

Hugo said again that this was all wrong, and not only that, it was also too soon. He hadn't finished the mission! He hadn't done his hero thing yet!

"I have every confidence that you will,

Lieutenant," said Mr. Ford in that low, pleasant, echoey speech-teacher, Sunday-school way he had of speaking.

Hugo took off running again through the water and the weeds.

The girl was hit. It caused her skirt to rise up, and Hugo could see everything she had — she was wearing no underwear — as she fell down into the water right in front of him.

He leaped to assist her and, ignoring his own wounds and without regard to his own safety and with conspicuous gallantry and intrepidity, he threw himself on her in order to protect her until help arrived.

Then President Ford came and started yanking at Hugo's left arm. "Now, that's enough, Lieutenant Cunningham," he said. "You have done your heroic act. That's enough. I have already given you your Silver Star. That's enough, Lieutenant. Get up off of her. Now, right now. That's an order, Lieutenant Ronald Derby Cunningham. What are you doing to her, Lieutenant? I order you to stop doing that. It is so un-Michigan. I'm going to tell Emily and your mother and your Sunday-school teacher, Lieutenant."

John Wayne and Van Heflin pulled Hugo off the woman marine.

Hugo ran away, searching desperately for

his lost sketch pad so he could draw a cartoon of his experience. . . .

It was at that moment that Hugo woke up. He sat straight up in bed.

His face was sweating profusely; his body felt like it was on fire. He saw — and felt — that one particular part of his body that had been most aroused.

He was truly embarrassed, and so grateful that he was all alone.

It was four-forty-five in the morning. He tried to go back to sleep but then got up and browsed through the thousands of cuff links that were up for auction on eBay. There were several with marine emblems, but he decided not to bid on any of them now. Not tonight.

He finally lay back down sometime after eight o'clock and fell asleep the second his head hit the pillow.

That was a terrible thing to do, because he didn't wake up until after nine-thirty.

# Two

He couldn't even remember the last time he had been late to work.

Except when sick or on vacation, Hugo was always — *always* — there before nine-forty-five A.M., fifteen minutes before opening, no matter the weather or any other calamity or circumstance. He was helped by the fact that he walked to work each morning, so he was never the victim of the unpredictable and often chaotic Washington traffic and weather.

This morning, dressed in a light brown 60 wool/40 rayon suit, he ran those twelve blocks over to and then down Eighteenth Street to L, shaving with his cordless Norelco razor and sticking a pair of gold National Security Council staff cuff links in his blue broadcloth dress shirt as he went.

He had looked for a taxi, but there were none to be found. There never were in Washington, except, he had read in the *Post,* at Reagan National Airport, where there were hundreds lined up. Hugo never understood why some of them didn't come downtown, where all the people were.

He stepped through the employee side entrance on Nineteenth Street at 10:07 A.M. The modest one-story store had been the Nash Brothers address in Washington since 1918. The public entrance on L Street had been unlocked by Jackson Dyer, the manager. Customers were coming in.

Hugo Marder was not only seven minutes late, Hugo Marder was puffing and sweating and exhausted — from the run, the sleeplessness, the Ronald Derby Cunningham nightmare. He was also mortified.

Jackson Dyer, already out on the sales floor, gave Hugo a noncommittal wave but said nothing. Nobody said anything to Hugo. Everybody was busy, sure, but somebody should have greeted him. His first time ever being late, and nobody said anything!

He was sure Robert would have, but Robert was down in front in his shoe section, busy with customers. Hugo recognized one as a senator from Montana or someplace out west. Robert Masefield was the best man on men's shoes Hugo had ever known. Hugo also considered Robert a friend, the best he had among his sales-associate colleagues. There was a playful irreverence to Robert that Hugo enjoyed and envied.

Jackson Dyer was also a friend, but in a different way. He was an honest and honorable, if ambitious, man who could be trusted. Nash Brothers, at least, trusted him to run their most important store in the world's most important city. That was good enough for Hugo. But Jackson was young, in his mid-forties, and he was the boss; technically, at least. Nash Brothers tried hard to keep their sales associates thinking they were answerable to a higher power than real people, to see themselves as the spiritual as well as the practical backbone of this famous retail institution. They were taught to answer first and foremost to the ideals that were born when the first Nash Brothers store opened on Madison Avenue 112 years ago. Or, as the senior man who'd trained Hugo had said, "Your main taskmasters will always be yourself and your own sense of excellence. No one has a superior at Nash Brothers. We are all superior people selling superior merchandise to superior customers. Superior is not just our middle name. It is all of our names."

Hugo would do his talking about his — no, *Ronald Derby Cunningham's* — Silver

Star with Robert. They were near the same age — Hugo was fifty-four, Robert, fifty-six — and they lunched together, traded customer stories, and even discussed events outside the store, most particularly the 9/11 attacks and then the UN debate and other events in the buildup to the Iraq invasion. Robert was also one of the few people in Washington with whom Hugo had ever discussed his early ambition to be a cartoonist, to maybe have a comic strip in the newspapers.

Robert was a Turk from Cyprus and had been a diplomat, a member of the Turkish foreign service, before coming to Nash Brothers. Robert was his real name, but Masefield was not. His real last name was something Turkish that he had changed to Masefield after the Turk army invaded Greek-majority Cyprus in 1974 and annexed — by force — the northern part of the island nation. Then a deputy in the Turkish embassy in Washington, Robert had immediately resigned in protest of the brutal invasion, which caused much death and suffering among the Greeks who got in the way. Robert officially immigrated to the United States and became Masefield, then, eventually, a naturalized U.S. citizen.

There were at least a dozen customers on

the floor. Several were in men's suits, sport coats, and slacks. A couple were over looking at shirts and ties. The rest were scattered about, including the three or four who were with Robert and his colleague in shoes.

Talking to Robert would have to wait. Business was always first.

Hugo approached a Call, a lone male customer who was looking through 42R suits. All of the other sales associates were busy. The rotation didn't matter when the store was this busy. Everybody took what he could handle as fast and as efficiently as possible, making sure to give preference to See Yous. Hugo saw no See Yous for him, though Dalton Andrews, the former cabinet officer and Washington eminence, was due later this morning.

Calls were customers who walked in cold; See Yous were repeats who made appointments or came in to do business with a particular sales associate.

"These are so much more expensive than in your outlet stores," said the Call as Hugo approached to offer assistance.

Hugo said nothing. What he thought but did not say was: I hate those outlet stores! I hate what they are doing to our quality way of doing things. Why should anyone come to us and pay the full $695 price for our top-of-the-line suit when he can drive to some mall outside Williamsburg or Leesburg, Virginia, or Martinsburg, West Virginia, and buy the same item for $395? The way the fools who are running us and the others like us with their catalogs and outlets, the days for personalized merchandising of high-quality clothing may very well be on the way out. And all of us with it!

"I think I'll pass for now," said the man, who had the uncreased, unpressed appearance and manner of an arms-control thinker. He walked away and out of the store, presumably to drive directly to Williamsburg, Leesburg, or Martinsburg.

Hugo moved to assist a pair of thirty-ish male lawyers who paid full price, and loved it, for two suits each plus an array of shirts and ties to go with them. Hugo's advice was solicited and accepted on every item. The lawyers told him proudly that they had just settled some litigation out of court, quite favorably to their clients, and thus to them. They said that instead of breaking out the caviar and champagne, they had elected to break out the American Express cards and buy some new clothes. They were the kind of people who were at the heart of what was called "the dessert" at Nash Brothers. The regulars — the See Yous — paid the bills, but it was the desserts such as these two Calls who paid the bonuses.

A woman in some sort of uniform was next. She was over in ties, first going through the bright patterns and then turning to more conservative plains. "I want something for my father — his birthday," she said to Hugo. He immediately decided that anything over a hundred dollars would not work for her. She was an attractive woman of possibly fifty. She had perfectly coiffed short brown hair, nice lips, small nose, smooth skin, ample figure. Her immaculately tailored two-piece gray uniform, Hugo saw now, was that of an airline employee. The small gold wings over her left breast pocket said GREAT LAKES AIRWAYS. A matching gold name tag over the other pocket said MELINDA CONWAY.

"Are you a pilot?" Hugo asked, suspecting she was not but might not mind being mistaken for one. It was part of the natural act of making a customer feel important. There was suddenly more going on here than that, and it accelerated when he noticed she was not wearing a wedding ring.

"No, no," said Melinda Conway, though she clearly enjoyed the suggestion. "I work at our downtown ticket office, over at the Ritz-Carlton."

Hugo moved her to the Jim Thompson–brand silk ties from Thailand. They had a good name, a good feel, but were not *that* expensive. He took a couple from the rack, folded them into faux knots, and held them against his own chest.

Melinda Conway studied, smiled, and then shook her head at both. Hugo grabbed another, bright red with small yellow elephants, outlined in black.

"That's it," she said.

He praised her taste, took her Master-Card, escorted her to a nearby checkout station, and, within a few minutes, had her and her father's new tie on her way.

Hugo had been attracted to Melinda Conway, but he was sure she'd left the store not knowing anything of the kind, having come and gone from his life only as a satisfied Call. Since his divorce from Emily, he still hadn't gotten back into the swing of knowing how to either transmit or receive signals of potential romantic interest. He had never been particularly good at it anyhow. His drawing aside, he sometimes thought the only thing he did well was sell men's clothes. And that was not enough.

It was nearly eleven o'clock. Almost an hour had gone by, and Hugo had not had a chance to even exchange looks with Robert, much less words.

There was a lull in the traffic. On Hugo's signal, Robert joined him in the rear of the store.

"Your tardiness this morning, Sir Hugo, has been noted by the Great Nash Brothers God of Menswear, both under and outer," Robert teased. "I fear, sir, that your very being as a purveyor of both double- and single-breasted suits is in dire jeopardy."

Hugo fought off a laugh. "Lunch today?" he said. "I have something important — personal — to discuss with you. Seriously."

Robert said, "Seriously? I hope and pray that you have impregnated a woman. If the issue to come from it is a male, we can sign him up now as a Nash Brothers sales associate of the future — like they do at Sidwell Friends or National Cathedral, Harvard or Yale."

"No, no. It's not that."

"I'm so sorry. Failure to impregnate is almost as serious as being late for work. Please tell me that you are at least *thinking* about impregnating a woman?"

Hugo gave in and rewarded Robert with a quiet laugh.

Robert, educated mostly in Britain, spoke English precisely and with a slight British accent. He had told Hugo that he'd chosen

Masefield for his last name partly because it began with an M, as did his real Turk Cypriot name, but mostly because he had always admired the work of the British poet John Masefield.

Robert was in a solid charcoal-brown suit. Unlike Hugo, he was tall and trim. His skin and hair were dark, and he had a thin mustache. Hugo's dark blond hair was thinning fast; his face was mustache-less, and his skin was cream white, except in the summertime, when occasionally — and very carefully — he let the sun put some color in his cheeks. His father had died of skin cancer, and the melanoma had started in his face, presumably from the sunburn he got working as a lineman for Michigan Bell.

"I have thought and done what is required to impregnate a woman," replied Hugo, deciding to play along with Robert, up to a point. "But I have never done so with that end result in mind."

Robert clicked his heels together and bowed stiffly from the waist. "I salute you, Sir Hugo, for your derring-do willingness to do what is required to impregnate."

Hugo decided this was not the time to give Robert the boring truth of his impregnation situation. It was simply that Emily had said on their second date, back in Big Rapids, that she had no interest in having children, at least until she had established herself in politics. Hugo, who hadn't really thought much about it, had agreed. The subject hadn't come up again by the time Emily left him, so she could devote her entire self to being a legislative assistant to her Republican congressman from Michigan. "I think I'm married to my job," she had said in her departure announcement after coming home very late at least thirty or so straight workdays, including Saturdays and Sundays. "I'd say I'll miss you," Hugo had replied, "but you can't miss what you've never really had, can you?" He was fairly pleased with himself for that spontaneous comeback.

Hugo and Robert were standing together in the rear of the store by the suits but facing the door. Always face the front, was the cardinal rule. Talk to anyone you wish, including someone on the phone, but always stay alert to who is coming in and out of the store. Be ready to move toward them, to help them, to service them, to sell them one or more of our quality goods . . .

They watched together with pleasure as Dalton T. Andrews, one of Hugo's most important See Yous, walked through the front door.

41

■ ■ ■ ■

As Hugo saw it, working at Nash Brothers had many advantages — "perks," they were called in the common language of commerce — that had nothing to do with health insurance, pensions, or terrific discounts on quality clothes and accessories. They were the kind and quality of the customers.

George Bush — the father — had bought his clothes here from the time he came to Washington as a Texas congressman. So had Al Gore and Bruce Babbitt and Lawrence Eagleburger. Many senators — Sam Nunn, David Pryor, and John Warner, in particular — were also regular customers. So were many famous men's wives who came in search of suitable gifts for their husbands. While most of the prominent people knew Hugo Marder only by regular sight, place, and function rather than by name or person, that was more than plenty. It was identity enough for Hugo — and more, he figured, than most people ever had, even in Washington.

But the man coming into the store now did know his name *and* face. Dalton T. Andrews had been an adviser to Democratic presidents, an ambassador, a special Middle

East negotiator, and, most important, secretary of defense before he settled back into his prestigious law firm.

It was just after eleven-fifteen, the time Mr. Andrews's assistant had said Mr. Andrews would be coming. He was alone, as always. Even when he was a cabinet officer, he had shopped by himself, insisting that his security men stay mostly out of sight.

"Hugo, I have an itch for a sport coat — something wild, loud, inappropriate — something to get my mind off the awful decision to go it alone in Iraq," he said, his voice still firm, as were his walk, his tall frame, and the part down the center of his full head of wavy gray hair. At seventy-eight, he remained a presence, a man who filled up a room. What was the connection between his impressive appearance and his impressive list of accomplishments? To Hugo's observation, big, handsome, deep-voiced, and, yes, well-dressed men seemed to do a lot better than short, ugly, squeaky ones in cheap or inappropriate clothes. That was part of what life was all about, and not just here in Washington.

Thoughts such as these had increasingly brought Hugo to consider the fact of his own presence. He, Sir Hugo, had only the *clothes* of a man of accomplishment.

Mr. Andrews had been a 46L when he first became Hugo's customer fifteen years ago. Now he was a 44R, mostly because his body had settled a bit. His line about a sport coat that was wild, loud, and inappropriate was a joke, of course. Nash Brothers sold nothing like that, and he wouldn't have bought such a thing if they did.

Hugo escorted Mr. Andrews to the sport coats and, within a few seconds, realized that he had not really come to buy anything in particular. Mr. Andrews was there to look, possibly to pass some idle time, to do something outside the office. Hugo was good at turning a Looker into a Buyer. But he would never try anything like that on Mr. Andrews. If he or any other See You wanted guidance toward an item, he would ask for it.

"Sir, how does one find out what a certain individual did in the military to win his Silver Star medal?" Hugo asked Mr. Andrews.

There had been no preplanned decision to say this. It had just popped out. As a hard, general rule, Hugo never brought up personal matters to a customer, no matter how long or friendly the relationship. He had seen more than one Nash Brothers colleague step over the line to ask for a reference letter ("Sir, my daughter is applying early decision to William and Mary, and I noticed that you are on their board of trustees . . .") or free legal advice ("Sir, I know your law firm is above mundane matters like this, but I was wondering how one goes about suing his landlord for not fixing the air-conditioning . . .").

"The citations for all medals like that are a matter of public record," said Mr. Andrews with only a glance at Hugo as he continued to skim his fingers over a Harris tweed three-button with a hint of dark gray and a quiet maroon stripe. Hugo knew for a fact that Mr. Andrews already had two Harris tweeds that were of a similar cut, style, and coloring.

Hugo waited for Mr. Andrews to say something else. When he didn't, Hugo said, "How does one go about looking at that record for a particular person, Mr. Andrews?"

"Write down his name, his branch of service, and his war on a piece of paper," Mr. Andrews said. "I'll see what I can do."

Hugo quickly went over to the checkout desk, took a sheet of Nash Brothers notepaper, and wrote, "Ronald Derby Cunningham. Marine Corps. Vietnam."

Mr. Andrews took the note and began

45

moving toward the door. He paused, looked at what Hugo had written, and stuck it in a coat pocket. "Checking out somebody's I-was-a-hero story, Hugo? There was a movie in the fifties about a guy who wore somebody else's Navy Cross lapel pin. Edmund Gwenn, I think, played the man. You ever see it?"

Hugo said he hadn't.

"There really are a lot of people out there wearing lapel buttons and even ribbons for medals they didn't win, that's for sure," added Mr. Andrews. "It's a most common of crimes — call it a sickness. Remember the Boorda case?"

"Yes, sir," Hugo said.

"You've probably seen a lot worse and never knew it," said Mr. Andrews as he departed.

Hugo definitely knew Boorda was the admiral, the head of the U.S. Navy, who had been exposed for allegedly wearing an unauthorized combat V — for valor — on his Bronze Star ribbon. Reporters for one of the newsmagazines had asked him about it and, faced with what he clearly expected to be some torturous public humiliation and disgrace, Boorda blew his brains out.

Hugo had read in *The Washington Post* about similar cases of the "sickness" among men — did it affect only men? — that had caused them to pose as the heroes they never were. There had been an episode about a well-known historian who had lied to his students about having been a Vietnam combat veteran. And there was a professional football coach who, like the history professor, had used phony stories of his nonexistent war experiences to psych up his players. A congressman claimed in his campaign literature to have been a Navy Seal in Vietnam rather than the Norfolk-only active-duty navy reservist he really was. A Palestinian intellectual had been outed for having manufactured an early life of woe and abuse at the hands of the Israelis.

Hugo also knew exactly what Mr. Andrews meant by his additional comment. He was talking about what Hugo himself had done the evening before — the wearing of an unearned medal lapel pin.

Hugo had seen hundreds of such pins in the course of selling clothes to prominent men of Washington. Some were tiny red and maroon ribbons and rosettes that, Hugo quickly learned, came from foreign governments, primarily the French. But most were the metal replicas of the ribbons for the Purple Heart and the Bronze Star, as well as the Silver Star. Hugo always made a comment to the customer, either saying something simple, such as "I honor your achievement, sir," or even asking how and in what war the man had won the medal or award. Without exception, they relished the attention and the question. Hugo agreed with Johnny Zorba, the gyro man, that they had a perfect right to advertise their extraordinary achievements.

Hugo's most stunning experience with this kind of thing was a Call — a delightfully gregarious gray-haired man with a stiff right leg — who had come in with an emergency need of a dark blue suit to wear that evening to an informal dinner at the White House. He said he had misread the invitation and flown in from someplace in Arizona with only a yellowish-tan-checked sport coat to wear. As Hugo inspected the coat, confirming that it would definitely not work that evening, he noticed a light blue rosette in the lapel that was of a type he had never seen before. He assumed it was French, but when he asked the Call, the man smiled and said, "It's the rosette for the Medal of Honor."

Hugo had never seen such a thing. Over the next forty-five minutes, while he waited for the Nash Brothers tailor to alter the man's new suit, Hugo listened to the harrowing story of what the customer had done to win the nation's highest military honor. A fighter pilot in Vietnam, he'd been shot down shortly after the war began, taken prisoner by the North Vietnamese, who, because he became the American prisoners' main leader, had beaten and tortured him. Also, during one terrible stretch, he was kept in solitary confinement over three years.

Now, as Hugo moved toward a Call who had just come in, he wondered if that earlier prison story had been a lie. Could the man have bought that rosette as Hugo had bought the Silver Star? No, no, not that man. He was authentic. No phony could have told the stories he'd told. Besides, the San Diego voice had said it was illegal to traffic in Medals of Honor. But what about rosettes?

And what about all of the others? Had some — any — of those distinguished Nash Brothers customers of Hugo's bought their lapel ribbons and buttons rather than won them?

Sam Springwell, Hugo's main sales trainer, who was a Battle of the Bulge veteran and now retired from Nash Brothers, had warned, "Figure fifty-fifty. Half of them earned what's in their lapel, the others didn't."

Several weeks after Sam told Hugo this, a Call came in wearing a Purple Heart lapel button. He told Hugo he'd gotten hit at the Battle of the Bulge. Hugo motioned for Sam to come over, and within a few minutes and questions, it became clear the man was a fake. Neither Sam nor Hugo had exposed him. Business was business.

Hugo now thought of others, particularly a former senator from Utah, a See You, who wore a Bronze Star lapel button. He'd said he had been an army rifleman in Korea and nearly frozen to death. True or false?

"May I help you, sir?" Hugo said now to the Call, a well-dressed, prosperous-looking man in his fifties. Hugo immediately spotted a tiny gold Marine Corps globe-and-anchor emblem in his coat lapel.

"I need to look at a suit — something dark, maybe with a stripe — that I can wear year-round," said the man. "Except when it's really hot or really cold."

In a few minutes, Hugo had the coat of a 42R Nash Brothers' Premium Class suit on the man. It was dark blue, almost black, with a heavy gray pinstripe. "Perfect," said the Call. In a few more minutes, he also said "Perfect" about a charcoal-gray suit and a tuxedo, and a few minutes after that, about a brown-and-gold-checked sport coat and two pairs of short-pleat slacks, four traditional straight-collar, button-cuff white dress shirts, and five ties of varying styles and colors. The total sale, handled by the Call with an American Express platinum card, came to $3,550.

It was, if Hugo could have been a bit boastful, the performance of a Nash Brothers master. The man — who had said he was a Ford Motor Company executive from Detroit, catching up on some clothes buying — initially asked only to look at a suit. But he left with two suits, a tux, and much, much more. What Hugo had done was based on another of the Nash Brothers assumptions: Nobody ever really comes in to buy one of anything. It is up to the skilled and experienced sales associate to make sure that does not happen. If it does, it is considered the failure of the sales associate. Melinda Conway didn't count. All she wanted was a necktie for her father. To have tried to push her to buy something else would have been a mistake.

Hugo's delight and satisfaction with his own performance with this marine Call were enhanced, of course, by the fact that, with his 6.5 percent commission, he would make $230.75 on the sale. He knew that without using a calculator or doing any math on paper, because he had learned to figure quickly in his head what 6.5 percent was of just about everything.

"You a former marine?" Hugo asked when the transaction was finally completed.

The man smiled and stiffened, almost as if being ordered to stand at attention. "That's right."

"That must be a great thing to be."

"There's nothing better."

"When were you in?" Hugo persisted.

"Vietnam, toward the end. I was an infantry officer. No combat, though."

"Did you happen to come across a marine lieutenant named Ronald Derby Cunningham?"

The Call thought, then said, "It's been a while, but the name doesn't ring any bells. The Corps is small, but not that small, I guess. What outfit was he in?"

Outfit? "I don't know."

"I was in Three-Nine — the Third Battalion, Ninth Marines. Was he related to you?"

"Oh, no. Just an acquaintance. He won the Silver Star."

"I won nothing but an experience that changed my life and membership in the greatest fraternity among men there is," said the Call. "And, as always, they're the first to be in harm's way in Iraq."

Hugo concluded the man was legit, a real former marine. At least he sure *seemed* like one. Was there any way to tell for sure?

Hugo said thanks for the business and, by handing out his business card, tried to turn the Call into a See You. "Keep me in mind when you're next in Washington and have the need for clothes," he said. "Ask for me."

"I will, thanks. Were you in the military?"

Hugo's mouth actually made a reflex movement toward forming the word "yes." But he stopped in time to simply shake his own head and the Call's right hand.

Hugo and Robert had picked up premade sandwiches, chips, and cold drinks from a carry-out counter at a semi–Middle Eastern soup and deli place on M Street.

Now they were sitting side by side on a bench in the bright, warm sunshine at the pocket-size park at Connecticut and N Street.

Feeling like a bad boy confessing to his mother, Hugo told Robert about the Silver Star medal, how, after watching the Wizards, the worst basketball team in history, fall behind as usual, he had gone to his desktop computer and clicked on eBay and begun a search for a *Star Wars*–related birthday present for his fifteen-year-old nephew. While shortening the possibilities — the original list contained 13,488 items — he had typed "silver" in front of "star wars" and hit "Search" again.

"But in the click-click process, I somehow hit a wrong key and deleted the word 'wars.' So what came up were the listings for 'silver star'— only 329 items. As I was about to correct my mistake by retyping 'wars' and trying again, my eye fixed on the third item on the list: 'Vietnam War Silver Star Medal — Named, Numbered — in Original Case.' On instinct, I clicked my mouse on the entry to open its full page on my screen —"

"Easy on the minutiae, Sir Hugo," said Robert, holding up his right hand. "My two teenage boys talk in computer speak, and it's not even my fifth language."

Hugo jumped to the end of the story. "Only one minute and twenty-four seconds remained in the auction. In a flash, without really thinking, I bid. Several more seconds passed, and I had bought a Silver Star medal set for eighty-five dollars, plus shipping and insurance."

There was now a look of bemused confusion on Robert's face. He said, "Please, Sir Hugo, tell me what is wrong with what you did? The world is full of good citizens who own and collect military medals —"

Hugo interrupted him and, again with much detail, told Robert about Johnny Zorba, the free gyro, and the fraudulent stroll up and down Connecticut Avenue with the Silver Star lapel pin in his coat.

It was clear, when he finished, that Robert still didn't quite understand Hugo's problem, his confession, his concern. So Hugo told much of it again, emphasizing that, for a while yesterday evening, he had posed not only as a marine but as a war hero, which seemed particularly unseemly in the post–9/11/Iraq world of real heroes, and also, that he felt dishonest and dirty even owning another man's Silver Star medal.

"Let me tell you about heroes, Sir Hugo," Robert said with no hint of satire. This was serious.

Robert said he had come home from college in England to a worsening of the historical tensions and tragedies between Cyprus's Greek and Turkish populations. While he was wondering if he had the courage to fight, to be a hero for his country, his father had told him a story about two young Turk Cypriots.

"They were both from the same family, the same village, the same soul. Both were physically and mentally strong, both went to the mountains to fight the Greeks. One was sent with a group of fighters to the left side of a hill, the other to the right side. On the left, there came a horrendous attack from the enemy, and the young man responded with heroism. He single-handedly killed more than twelve of the enemy and carried ten of his own wounded to safety. On the right, there was no attack. The young man on that side of the hill had no opportunity to show heroism."

Robert stopped talking. He smiled at Hugo. "You know what's coming, don't you?"

"I do, I do," said Hugo.

"Yes, one young man returned to his village and to a life as an ordinary man. The other, who was his friend, his equal, returned as a hero. They were blood brothers, men who revered each other, but after their return to their different welcomes, they moved as apart as if they were mountains on either side of a large valley. One lived on his side of the valley as if he were a saint. People parted as before God when he came down the main street for water or for a sandwich or for a newspaper — or for a beautiful woman of his choice."

Hugo interrupted to say there was no need

to tell him about the other man. He knew what had happened. "He got stuck with a plain wife and an ordinary life."

"Precisely," said Robert. "His daily existence was no different, no more special, than that of the man who wrung the necks of the chickens or slathered grease on the axles of carts."

Hugo nodded.

But Robert added, "The only difference between the two young men was opportunity. Had the other gone to the left, it is most likely — probable, beyond much doubt — that he would have been the one to have acted heroically."

Hugo got the point of the story but not exactly how it spoke to his situation.

Robert looked out at the traffic on Connecticut Avenue. Then he turned back to Hugo. "So, there you have it, Hero-in-Waiting Hugo. The Truth According to Robert of Nash Brothers. *Wear the medal.*"

When Hugo didn't respond, Robert quickly said, "For the record, I assume you did not serve in the U.S. military?"

Hugo nodded.

"Did you burn your draft card or escape to Canada?"

"No, but I didn't volunteer for the marines, as I'd planned to do since I was a kid, and I used college deferments to keep from being drafted. Six or seven of my buddies from high school did end up going to Vietnam. One of them died."

"Now you wish you had become a marine and gone to Vietnam?"

"Yes," said Hugo.

"So you want to be what they are and you are not . . ." Robert stopped and told Hugo to look at the woman who had just passed them, heading toward the intersection at Connecticut and N. She was dark-skinned, well dressed, about forty, and carrying a large shiny black purse over one shoulder.

"Watch, she's stopping for the light. Now look across Connecticut there, at the young man who is waiting to come across this way — opposite her."

Hugo looked.

"Now, wouldn't you estimate that they will pass each other in the middle of the street?" Robert asked.

Hugo agreed.

"All right, let's imagine that as they pass each other, the young man grabs the woman's purse, jerks it loose from her shoulder, and races away. What would you do?"

"I'd run out there, head him off."

"He's doing it!" Robert said. "He's reaching for her purse!"

Hugo jumped up. His sandwich fell to the ground. So did his package of chips and can of Diet Coke.

Robert pulled Hugo back down. "No, no. Watch them. I was mistaken."

Hugo saw the woman and the man meet in the middle of Connecticut Avenue. Nothing happened. Neither even looked at the other.

Said Robert, still seated on the bench, "You have just proved my thesis. You're a born marine, Hugo. All that lapel pin did was to finally unlock that man of valor, that brave man of courage, you have always been. What did you do with the Silver Star pin?"

"I put it back in the case with the medal and ribbon and stuck the case way back in my downstairs closet," said Hugo. "That's where they will stay forever."

Robert said, "You have heard the Truth According to Robert of Nash Brothers. *Wear* the blessed medal, Sir Hugo."

Less than an hour after lunch, a young paralegal/messenger from Mr. Andrews's law firm came into the store and handed Hugo a business-size white envelope.

Hugo took a deep breath and opened it while keeping an eye on the door for any of his See Yous. There were seven associates working this afternoon, so it would be a while before his turn came for another Call.

There was a handwritten cover note from Mr. Andrews that said, "Your man definitely earned his medal, Hugo. He was no phony marine hero."

Below Mr. Andrews's signature was a kind of P.S.: "I've been told this kind of information is available to anyone on the Internet. Also, the Navy Cross movie was called *Something for the Birds*."

Clipped to the note was a xeroxed copy of a document, headed with the words SECRETARY OF THE NAVY.

Below that, it read:

The President of the United States takes pleasure in presenting the SILVER STAR MEDAL to:

**Second Lieutenant**
**Ronald Derby Cunningham**
**071278, United States Marine Corps**

CITATION

For conspicuous gallantry and intrepidity in action while serving as a Platoon leader, 1st Platoon, Company B, 1st Battalion, 9th

Marines, 3rd Marine Division, in action against enemy aggressor forces in Vietnam on 5 December 1969. While on patrol forward of the main line of resistance, a squad from Lieutenant Cunningham's platoon came under an intense volume of small arms fire. Several of his Marines were killed or wounded. Lieutenant Cunningham led a mission to retrieve the dead and wounded. He was immediately wounded in his legs and right arm. Despite his wounds, he rallied his platoon and then, without regard for his own condition and his own safety, covered another wounded Marine with his own body until help arrived. He supervised the evacuation of that Marine and others wounded in the conflict. Through his initiative, courageous actions, and complete dedication to duty, Lieutenant Cunningham reflected great credit upon himself and upheld the highest traditions of the Marine Corps and the United States Naval Service. Lieutenant Cunningham entered the federal service from James Summit, Missouri.

For the President<br>The Secretary of the Navy

What Hugo had dreamed the other night was eerily similar to what had happened to

Ronald Derby Cunningham.

Hugo waited for the early-afternoon lull before showing the letter to Robert, who read it without comment and handed it back.

"So what should I do?" Hugo asked.

"I have already spoken to that, sir, with My Truth."

"Maybe I should try to find the man — if he is still alive and is to be found — and return his Silver Star? Or maybe see if he has family who would like to have it?"

Robert smiled, cocked his head, and said, "That medal is yours now — not his."

Hugo said nothing. He was thinking that very thing and hating himself for doing so.

So he said it. "God, I wish I was a former marine. I wish I had won that Silver Star for gallantry in action."

"Oh, Sir Hugo," said Robert. "I wish, I wish, I wish. There is no more time for wishes. If you want to be somebody else, do it! Be it now!"

He stuck his right forefinger gently against Hugo's left breast, as if putting a medal there.

*No, no! It's not that I am not satisfied with my life. I am completely satisfied with my life . . .*

These words were part of a conversation

Hugo had with himself on the walk home that evening.

He couldn't remember ever thinking that he didn't like himself or the life he was leading. Yes, he sometimes still wished that his drawing dream had worked out. But he was not only comfortable in his position at Nash Brothers, he was proud of it. Most of the time, at least. But was he kidding himself? Was there a life's moment of excitement he had missed? A revelation that had zipped by him? No. Definitely not. If anything like that had happened, it must have been a creeping, crawling kind of thing that began — maybe — after he and Emily came to Washington. Maybe it was a fever that had risen within him almost imperceptibly, until now.

Until he suddenly decided he wanted to become a former marine who had won the Silver Star?

Maybe he was losing it. Maybe he was a nutcase. Maybe he should go talk to a shrink. Are there shrinks who specialize in fifty-four-year-old men who suddenly decide to become phony marines?

From the beginning, Hugo had considered himself a happy person, living a life that was pleasant, reasonably rewarding, and satisfying. His father, Rick Marder, had worked for Michigan Bell since high school, made good money, and was considered a solid citizen in town. Newton was neither large nor prosperous enough to have layers of society. The bankers and the few lawyers taught Sunday school and attended Kiwanis and Rotary with store owners and shoe salesmen and, on occasion, Michigan Bell linemen. Among families, it was even more comfortable. Everyone was allowed to fit in, including Hugo and his mother, Sally, the wife of a telephone lineman.

Hugo had always said to Emily, and to himself, that he'd never longed to be rich and/or famous, to be the object of public worship. He had not ached to play shortstop for the Detroit Tigers or act in movies with Audrey Hepburn. He had not dreamed of discovering cures for dreaded diseases or even creating artistic masterpieces. His creative stirrings were all contained in his desire to be a cartoonist. This came directly from a teacher's praise for some cartoons he drew in sixth-grade art class. She praised his drawing skills, though, not his messages and/or jokes. That lack of something to say was the problem.

Earlier, when he was ten, during a school homeroom show-and-tell session, his friend Jason Aldrich brought down the house by declaring, "I'm going to be president of the

United States someday . . . or at least vice president, or, the very least, a United States senator . . . or the mayor of Newton."

Hugo and most of the other students laughed.

"I don't want your finger on no atombomb buttons," somebody said.

"That's fine, if you'll promise to pave all the streets in town with gold," kidded another.

Miss Litton, their homeroom teacher, told everyone to hush. "This is America," she said. "It's possible for anyone to grow up and be president — or anything else he wants to be."

This was 1959. There was no "or she" in the sentence spoken by Miss Litton, a tall, thin woman who wore her skirts almost down to her ankles and her pitch-black hair in a bob. Hugo always thought of her as old, but she was probably not more than thirty-five, if that. Some of the other boys had said they had wet dreams, thinking about the body that was under Miss Litton's long dresses. Hugo's imagination wasn't yet that advanced.

"Let's go around the room and see what each of you wants to be," said Miss Litton. "If not president, what?"

Two aspirations to be teachers and others

to be a preacher, a lawyer, a football coach, and a police detective had been expressed by the time it was Hugo's turn.

"A U.S. Marine," he said. He was about to add "or a cartoonist" when some kid squealed, "You?" in disbelief.

There was a slight rumble of agreement among some other classmates. Hugo heard one say, "The squirt thinks he's John Wayne." Hugo kept his head down so the redness he knew was beaming from his cheeks could not be seen.

"The squirt." Sometimes his dad called him "squirt," but that was different. There was no question he was small — the second or third shortest and lightest boy in his class. His mother kept telling him to just be patient, because boys grow at different rates and different times from girls and one another.

Miss Litton came to his rescue. "Now, now. If Jason can grow up to be president, Hugo can certainly grow up to be a marine." Hugo appreciated the thought but wished she had used some other phrase than "grow up." She had also said it in a way that seemed like she really meant growing up physically — getting bigger.

Then, to Hugo's relief, Miss Litton called on the girl who was next. "A nurse," said the girl, and the attention was off Hugo and his marine dream.

At that time, Hugo still had not even laid eyes on a real marine. His marine aspiration came mostly from the movies and from reading a comic book about marine sergeant John Basilone, an Italian-American kid from New Jersey who won the Medal of Honor at Guadalcanal in World War II. As far as Hugo knew, there were no marines in Newton. That was still the case when Vietnam came along.

The single Vietnam death was that of Jason Aldrich. He enlisted in the army when he was a sophomore at the University of Michigan at Ann Arbor, where he had majored in political science and economics. He was an A student who easily could have avoided service on his college deferment, but, on a weekend visit to Newton, he told Hugo that wouldn't work. "Draft-dodging won't look good on my political résumé later."

By then, being a marine was no longer a serious dream for Hugo, but Jason's declaration brought it back. Hugo, at college in Kalamazoo, was working toward no future résumé — no real goal other than to get a college degree, something neither of his parents had done.

"Want to go with me?" Jason asked Hugo that weekend.

"I'd go in the marines, not the army," Hugo said.

"That's okay. They're on the same side."

Hugo said he needed some time to think about it, and he went back to Kalamazoo.

Jason never made it to Vietnam. He volunteered for paratroop school and died in a practice jump at Fort Bragg, North Carolina. The lines on his parachute got twisted as he left the plane.

Hugo came home for Jason's funeral, which was held at the Methodist Church, with a burial at Newton's only cemetery and full military honors.

After the funeral, Hugo again thought about enlisting in the marines. Again he went back to Kalamazoo.

# THREE

When Hugo got home, he did not take the Silver Star case out of the closet, to look at the medal, the ribbon, and the lapel pin.

The next morning he considered a quick glance before walking out the front door. He resisted.

That evening, more rested and keenly aware of what was in the closet, he gave in — almost. He went as far as opening the closet door. But then he closed it and went about the business of making a grilled cheese — longhorn colby — sandwich and a bowl of soup, which he concocted with great artistry by combining the contents of a can of Campbell's tomato soup with water in a pan.

Over the following days, up to late Easter Sunday afternoon, he continued to fight and win the good fight. It called to mind Edgar Allan Poe's "The Tell-Tale Heart," which Hugo had read in high school, about a killer who couldn't escape the increasingly loud beating of a heart from below the wooden floor where he had hidden his victim's corpse.

Hugo at last gave in after watching the Wizards lose again to the San Antonio Spurs, for their eighth straight loss. He went to the closet and grabbed the case from its hiding place.

Within moments, that Silver Star pin was in the lapel of his pale blue long-sleeved sport shirt. But instead of exiting the red door for a stroll along Connecticut Avenue, he went to his computer. This was a private wearing, just for himself.

Soon he was browsing eBay's Marine Corps section.

There were more than sixteen hundred entries.

The first item he bid on was a pair of round silver cuff links with gold marine emblems.

The second was a 614-page 1968 edition of *The Marine Officer's Guide.* It had a BUY NOW price of thirty dollars, meaning if he was willing to go that high, he wouldn't have to wait the four days left on the auction.

He put his cursor on BUY NOW and single-clicked, then moved to PayPal, a method of paying for eBay items immediately through a secure transfer of bank funds. He added $12.50 for an expedited FedEx shipment.

Then he remembered Mr. Andrews's movie, the one about a man who wore another's Navy Cross lapel pin. *Something for the Birds.* Was that it? Yes. Starring Edmund Gwenn.

Hugo checked several VHS/DVD websites as well as eBay. There were write-ups of the movie, with the cast, director, and other details — black-and-white, eighty-one minutes long — but not only were no copies for sale, it appeared none had ever been made. The *TV Guide* site gave it only two stars but did say the movie was scheduled for two showings on the FOX Movie Channel in ten days. Hugo wrote down the date and times.

And then he was hungry. He thought, Why not try that House on the Klong, the fancy Thai place?

He shut down his computer, grabbed a dark blue blazer, transferred the Silver Star lapel pin to the coat, and headed for the red door.

Hugo was warmly welcomed by a gorgeous Asian woman in her early twenties. She was dressed in a multicolored brocade dress that went all the way to the floor. She didn't seem to notice his Silver Star lapel pin, which was understandable, since she was way too young and too Thai.

The hostess was politely concerned that he had no reservation. "Our door is open to all at all times," she said in a sweet, high voice. "But this is a most special situation tonight, and we have no available tables. You are not here for the Mr. Jim Thompson event, is that so?"

He told her that was so; he had just come in for a meal. She again expressed her regrets, and Hugo was about to leave when he noticed an elderly Thai man approaching.

"I see that you are leaving," said the man, who was small and almost effeminate. He had a smooth, distinguished smile on his face, and he was wearing a well-cut double-breasted black poplin suit, which, while not a Nash Brothers, Hugo figured was at least off-the-rack Neiman Marcus or Bloomingdale's quality, if not tailor-made. The man's dress shirt was white silk, and his tie, a Jim Thompson silk, was dark yellow, decorated with tiny light blue elephants. "I am so sorry that we are unable to accommodate you, sir. Normally, on Sunday evenings, we would have no problem, but

we are overflowing with customers tonight
. . ."

He stopped talking as his eyes fixed on
the Silver Star lapel pin. He pulled his feet
together, bowed his head slightly, and then
said, "It is an honor to have you in my
restaurant, sir." He nodded discreetly to the
Silver Star pin. "My apologies for my granddaughter."

After an order given only with his eyes,
the granddaughter took Hugo immediately
toward a table in the Phuket Boathouse, the
crowded main dining room in the center of
the restaurant. The decor was mostly nauti-
cal — boat propellers, white rope knots,
sailboat ensigns, large shells, and stuffed
fish, along with several framed eleven-by-
fourteen color photos of what was said to
be the original Phuket Boathouse back in
Thailand. There were also several small
bronze and porcelain statues of Buddha,
and photographs of Jim Thompson, the man
of silk who had built the real House on the
Klong.

Hugo caught a glimpse of a vaguely familiar face, a woman sitting at a table some
fifteen yards away on the other side of the
room. He knew her from somewhere, but
where? She smiled at him, and he smiled
back, but he didn't go over to her table. He

couldn't do that until he placed her. She seemed attractive — dark blond, done up — but it was hard to tell from this distance and in this light. She was with someone, who, from the rear, appeared to be a very large man.

Hugo followed the granddaughter-hostess, confirming that this restaurant was indeed doing unusually well for a Sunday evening, any evening. As best as he could see, his table really was the only vacant one left. Who had they been saving it for? Too bad for whoever it was.

But who *was* that woman over there? Had he recently met her?

"What a coincidence." And there she was, standing at Hugo's table, extending her right hand. "My father loved the Jim Thompson tie."

He stood up and took her hand. "I'm delighted. I had a feeling he would."

"It's another good coincidence to be here at this restaurant . . . you know, the Jim Thompson connection and all."

Hugo agreed. He was now at full recognition. This was the airline-woman Call. The one who . . . well, had interested him a bit. What was her name? Melinda? Yes, Melinda. Last name — Connelly . . . Conwell — Conroy. Conroy! Yes, Melinda Conroy.

Hugo seldom forgot the name of a customer.

Melinda Conroy was staring at Hugo's coat lapel. "You won the Silver Star?" she said, her voice rising with excitement. "My dad won a Silver Star in World War Two. He was a navigator on a B-29 that bombed Japan. What about you?"

"Marines — Vietnam," he said as softly as he could.

His mind was not on the Silver Star connection or on his lie. He was absorbed at the moment with how even more attractive she was here than she'd been at the store. She was wearing a dark satin tailored coat dress with a notch collar and button front. Her hair was relaxed, straight, fixed but not stiff.

"Do you come here often?" Hugo asked. He couldn't think of anything else to say!

"No, this is my first time." She pointed down at the menu the owner's granddaughter had left by his place. "Its story is all there on the back. Do *you* come here a lot?"

"First time for me, too. I live close by, though."

"I live out in Reston, near Dulles."

She looked away; Hugo looked away. There was nothing more to say. So she wrapped it up: "Well, have a nice dinner, and I'm glad you're a Silver Star, too — like my dad."

She departed in the direction of her table, and Hugo sat down again, his back to her. He kicked himself for not allowing his eyes to linger long enough for a quick peek at what she looked like from behind. He had been mostly a looker since he and Emily split, with only a handful of unremarkable liaisons in recent months.

He picked up the menu. It was covered with multicolored litho prints of small boats on lagoons and golden temples and white beaches and large elephants and exotically dressed Thai dancers. He thought he could have drawn these things as well as this. Maybe he should have tried to get a job illustrating restaurant menus.

And then he wondered about Melinda's age. She had seemed at least fifty at the store, but tonight she seemed younger, forty-five or so. Did she live in Reston with a husband, the guy with her tonight? Or was he her live-in lover? She wasn't wearing a wedding ring. Maybe he was only a casual acquaintance. Maybe she was divorced? But with children? Maybe the guy was her brother.

The genealogy of the restaurant was

indeed written on the back of the menu, the Jim Thompson story told first. He had come to Thailand at the end of World War II as an OSS officer and stayed to make a reputation and a fortune by developing the Thai silk industry. He also had been an early collector of very old Asian art and artifacts, which he displayed in a house he'd built from the various parts of old native homes on one of Bangkok's waterways, or klongs. Thompson, amid rumors of CIA and Vietcong and various other sinister connections, disappeared in 1967 while on a weekend holiday in the Central Highlands of Malaysia. No trace of him was ever found. The owner of this restaurant, then a poor Bangkok teenager, had served as a message runner for Thompson and his covert OSS operation. It was as a kind of memorial that the owner had named this restaurant after Thompson's Bangkok masterpiece residence.

A waiter came with a bottle of champagne and a single frosted glass. Except for the granddaughter, the restaurant was operated by an all-male cast. The waiters, each dressed in a white shirt, black no-pleat pants, and a thin tie, were young men of dark skin and black hair who could have passed for the hostess's twin brothers.

"It would honor me greatly, sir," said the elderly owner, appearing at Hugo's side, "if you would permit me to formally introduce myself and to present to you this champagne as my way of offering a toast to you, to your country and its friendship with my native land, the Royal Kingdom of Thailand."

Hugo rose.

"I am You Johnny at your service," said the owner, taking Hugo's hand and bowing slightly. "I have a long and difficult-to-pronounce name, but You Johnny was what Mr. Jim Thompson called me. 'Hey you, Johnny,' he would say. So that is what I have called myself ever since, when I am among Americans."

Hugo motioned for him to please have a seat at the table.

"No, no, but thank you, sir," said You Johnny. "I am here to serve, not to intrude. Also, we are most unexpectedly busy tonight, with many new faces as well as those of a few friends I invited to share this special evening. It was on this day, on Easter Sunday in the year 1967, that Mr. Jim Thompson disappeared. We will be noting it more appropriately with a unique delicacy in the due course of the evening."

He moved away. Hugo watched as he glided around and between the thirty or so tables in the room, visiting and laughing with the customers, filling water glasses and doing whatever else seemed necessary to keep everyone as happy as he appeared to be.

Hugo took a sip of the champagne, which was excellent, and continued reading the outside of the menu. It said Phuket was a town in a popular resort area on the south-west coast of Thailand that, among other glorious things, was used as a submarine drop-off spot for U.S. and British commandos sent to link up with the anti-Japanese resistance during World War II, with which the owner of the restaurant was affiliated. The Boathouse was a small hotel at Phuket that was known for its superb white-sand beach, exquisite Thai and European food, and "world-wise" clientele. The proprietor of the House on the Klong here on Connecticut Avenue in Washington, D.C., U.S.A., had, "with full permission and alliance," patterned the decor, food, style, and spirit of its central dining room after the original Phuket Boathouse.

The menu itself listed little food that appealed to Hugo. He finally decided on something called Pla Neung, which was described as being a fresh filet of large red snapper, steamed in Oriental apricot sauce with black bean, ginger, celery, onion, and shiitake mushrooms, topped with fried leeks. He ordered two spring rolls on the side.

And then, with no warning, Melinda Conway was standing by his table. Again he was on his feet. She said, "Are you alone? Please come and join my friend and me. We have only just ordered. My friend was a marine. He'd love to meet you."

Oh, God! No, no. I'm not ready — not yet.

He kicked himself for succumbing to the temptation of the Silver Star lapel pin. If he hadn't worn it, the owner of this crowded restaurant wouldn't have made a place for him, he never would have run into this Call, and this wouldn't be happening . . .

I'm not ready!

"My name, in case you forgot, is Melinda — Melinda Conway," she said, gently taking Hugo by the arm and moving him away from the table. Conway — not Conroy!

A waiter said he would follow with the champagne and two more chilled glasses.

Hugo saw Melinda Conway's companion, on his feet, waiting for them at their table. He was a very big man.

"I'm not sure I told you the other day, but I'm Hugo Marder," said Hugo as calmly as

80

he could manage.

He considered faking a sudden illness, falling to the floor after tripping himself or going to the restroom to gain some time to think.

"Hugo Marder. That has a really nice sound to it."

Nobody had ever said "Hugo Marder" had a really nice sound.

They were at her table, where busboys were working quickly to set another place. Melinda would be to his right, her former marine — *real* former marine — dinner companion on his left.

"Semper Fi," said the big man. "I'm Matt."

"Semper Fi," Hugo said. "I'm Hugo."

Matt, in his late forties, was over six feet tall, athletic, a perfect marine specimen. His suit, shirt, and tie, a mix of dark blues and bright whites, were Italian. Armani, possibly, but the fit was slightly loose, which probably meant he'd bought them at one of the dreadful outlet stores. There was no pin in his coat lapel.

"In Vietnam?" Matt asked, and nodded toward Hugo's Silver Star pin.

Hugo nodded. His head was racing with possible ways out — escapes. I'm not ready yet for this!

"When were you in the Corps?" Hugo asked Matt after they were all seated. Take the initiative. Interview *him*. Don't give him a chance to ask any questions.

"Early seventies — five years," said Matt.

Hugo felt Matt had something on his mind that had nothing to do with the marines. He kept looking around the restaurant and at his watch. He seemed jumpy, restless. Hugo took that to mean he wasn't particularly pleased that Melinda had asked Hugo to join them. Maybe it was something else. Whatever, Hugo was delighted for the distraction.

"What do you do now?" Hugo asked, determined to stay on the offensive.

"I'm in law enforcement," Matt said, his voice dropping to a near-whisper. "With a small federal agency — nothing that big. You?"

Hugo said much more about his job at Nash Brothers than Matt cared to know. In fact, Matt seemed to barely be listening to Hugo's talk about selling quality clothes to quality men.

"What marine outfit were you in?" Matt finally asked. At first Hugo, his mind still on his duties at Nash Brothers, looked down at his own suit and was about to explain the dark blue poplin material and English cut

. . . when he caught himself.

*Marine* outfit. That's what he was asking.

Hugo took what he believed to be the longest and deepest breath up to this point in his life before saying, "First Battalion, Ninth Marine Regiment."

"Oh, wow. One-Nine. The Walking Dead. Some outfit."

Hugo had no idea what Matt was talking about. He knew only that Ronald Derby Cunningham's unit was the First Battalion, Ninth Marine Regiment. Thank God I remembered. I forgot Melinda's last name, but not Cunningham's unit.

Hugo took a long sip of champagne.

"I was in Two-Six out of Lejeune. We went to the Mediterranean, and that was it. Nothing like what you had in Vietnam, that's for goddamn sure."

Hugo nodded.

"What was your MOS?" Matt asked.

MOS. Well, so much for my new life as a former marine, thought Hugo. He had not a prayer of an idea what such a thing as an MOS was, much less what his was. There was nothing in Cunningham's Silver Star citation about that.

Hugo considered choking on the champagne but decided he would simply ignore the question and change the subject. He made some comment on the unusual decor of the restaurant.

Matt, looking at the various images of Buddha around the place, said, "I'll bet you anything they're all hot as firecrackers. Swiping those things out of temples in Thailand and then selling them here and everywhere else in the world is one very big business."

Melinda said this restaurant brought back something her father had told her: Before the 20th Air Force began bombing targets in Japan from bases in China in 1944, many B-29s flew a practice raid on Bangkok. "Thailand, at Japan's insistence, had declared war on the United States, so it was considered okay. Because Bangkok was about the same distance from China as Japan, it made for a good practice run," she said. "Dad said he believed several thousand Thais were killed, and hundreds of buildings were destroyed. Did you know about that?"

Hugo wanted to hug her. For now, at least, the MOS question was lost.

"Sounds like more of that anti-American propaganda every foreigner puts out with one hand while putting his other out for aid," said Matt.

"My father did not put out propaganda,"

said Melinda with a noticeable frost. Hugo had observed no wedding band on Matt's left hand. Hugo was close to concluding that not only did they not live together or date regularly, they didn't even know each other very well. He was beginning to wonder what had brought the two of them together to have dinner this particular Easter Sunday. Did either or both have a special appreciation for Jim Thompson?

Melinda, full of energy and grace, changed the subject again to express her delight about the champagne, and particularly with the circumstances that had led it to be given to Hugo.

"We couldn't ever get my dad to wear his Silver Star pin out in public the way you do, Hugo," she said. "He had a pretty good life, as it was, but I always believed it could have been so much better if everyone he came in contact with knew immediately that he was a hero."

"It's all a matter of personal taste," said Matt. "I know a lot of guys who won medals in Vietnam who wouldn't think of going around wearing them in public."

"Well, that's their loss," said Melinda. "They could be drinking good free champagne, too."

Then Matt snapped to Hugo: "Your MOS.

You never told me your MOS."

"What was yours?" Hugo said back quickly.

"Oh-three — infantry. Recon."

Recon? Must be short for reconnaissance. Something special beyond just the infantry. "Infantry, that's what I was, too," Hugo said.

Matt gave him a hard stare. He seemed ready to ask another question when a grinning waiter slipped a small bowl of steaming soup in front of Hugo. It was dark brown, thick. "Mr. You Johnny's compliments. It is a very important soup — one of the most important in the world. A few are eating it tonight, and he wanted you to have some, too."

"What kind is it?" Hugo asked. Was it a form of chili? A fish stew? "What's it called?"

"It has no name, sir," said the waiter. "Mr. You Johnny eat it every year on this day to remember Mr. Jim Thompson."

The waiter disappeared, and Hugo picked up a spoon and put a tiny bit of the soup in it. He blew on it and then took a sip. It had a strong, tart taste — musty, different. Not fish, definitely not chili. But it was faintly meaty, beefy. Hugo moved the spoon back toward the bowl, intending to go for seconds. But then a hand came down on his wrist. It was Matt's. "It has a name," he said in a whisper. "It's called bear claw soup."

"What does that mean?" He paused before dipping the spoon again.

"It means the base ingredient is a claw chopped off a dead bear."

Hugo put the spoon down on the table and fought off throwing up — for real.

Then he felt something leather being slipped under the table toward him. It was a small black billfold-type case. Hugo opened it to a shiny gold badge on one side, an ID card on the other. The badge had U.S. at the top, under an eagle, then in a circle in the center, DEPARTMENT OF INTERIOR and FISH AND WILDLIFE SERVICE. Below that were the words SPECIAL AGENT. The card had a muglike shot of Matt and words that identified him as MATTHEW C. CO-LUMBIA, SPECIAL AGENT IN CHARGE — SPECIAL OPERATIONS.

"Matt's a kind of cop," Melinda whispered. "He's here tonight on business — he didn't tell me what, exactly. His girlfriend is a neighbor, but she was tied up tonight, so she asked if I would fill in as a kind of date —"

Then Matt said what sounded like "Go!" into his left coat sleeve. He stood and moved away from their table.

A voice rang out: "Ladies and gentlemen, may I have your attention, please!"

Hugo turned around to see a well-dressed young man standing in the center of the dining room, holding a small portable megaphone. "I am Special Agent Whitney of the U.S. Fish and Wildlife Service! Please do not be alarmed! Look around you! The people standing now are also law-enforcement officers!"

Hugo saw several people leaping to their feet at tables throughout the restaurant.

The man on the megaphone said, "We are involved in an official operation in connection with the Lacey Act, which forbids interstate trafficking in animal parts. Please remain calm and in your seats. Those of you who have been served a special bowl of soup, please do not eat, touch, or disturb the bowl or its ingredients in any way. That could constitute interfering with evidence in a federal criminal case, which is a felony and punishable by imprisonment and a fine. No one will get hurt if you —"

At that moment Melinda screamed. Hugo turned back toward her. A man had grabbed her from behind, one arm around her neck, the other holding a silver pistol to her head.

"Nobody does anything or this woman

die!" yelled the man. He was black-haired, dark-skinned, well dressed, around thirty. His eyes, bright and as dark as his hair, were lasered at Hugo.

Melinda's blue eyes, wide open and full of fear, were also fixed on him.

They flitted from Hugo's face to his coat lapel.

*You're a Silver Star hero, Hugo!* screamed her eyes to Hugo. *Do something!*

Hugo could not move. *I'm not ready yet!*

At that moment Matt lunged at the gunman. He grabbed the pistol butt in both hands. The man let go of Melinda but held tight to the gun. He fell backward, and Matt fell with him.

Hugo still didn't move.

Then some other men were there, helping Matt wrestle the gunman into handcuffs and his gun into harmless custody.

"Thank the good Lord for Matt," said Melinda, clearly saying also that there was absolutely no need to thank the good Lord or anyone else for Hugo Marder.

But it wasn't over.

Hugo heard yelling behind him. He swung around to see a man in a white chef's outfit standing in front of the door to the kitchen. He was holding a machine gun of some kind. He fired a burst of bullets. Matt lurched toward Melinda and yelled, "Down!"

She dropped to the floor facedown, and Hugo came down on top of her, his body spread-eagled to cover her up. It was a move he had seen Secret Service agents make in movies.

"Don't move, don't move," Hugo said to her. "You're going to be fine."

There were more shots fired, followed by the sounds of glass crashing and people pleading for their lives. Then more shots, more noise from shattering things, more panicked yells. Had the man killed some people? Was a massacre going on here? Who was this guy? The chef?

Melinda's body felt good, solid, under Hugo. His head was in her hair, which smelled of perfume. He was beginning to feel aroused. He couldn't believe it! A crazy man was shooting people, and maybe they were next, and he was turned on.

"Thank you," Melinda said softly in a tone now tinged with awe and admiration.

"I'm not ready yet," Hugo whispered to Melinda.

"Ready for what?"

Then everything went silent.

A man spoke: "I am in the kitchen with the man some of you know as 'You Johnny.'

He wants to talk to the officer in charge, and he wants the Silver Star man to come with him — for neutral protection."

"I am the senior agent present." It was Matt's voice. "That is the Silver Star man, down there on the floor on top of the woman. Hey, Hugo! Up and at 'em!"

Hugo eased off of Melinda and got to his feet.

The man waved his gun in a motion that said for Matt and Hugo to come with him. He must have been the one speaking a moment ago.

Hugo started walking toward the kitchen door, doing his best to scan the room for the blood and remains of the people this madman must have killed or mutilated. He saw nothing like that. Could he have fired only above people's heads?

Hugo visualized newspaper and television stories that would report his death here in this Thai restaurant, probably from machine-gun fire in the kitchen. He might be identified as a failed cartoonist, but surely as a sales associate at Nash Brothers. That was fine. But just as surely, the stories would also say he was a former marine who had won the Silver Star. Melinda would be quoted about how he'd won the medal in Vietnam, Matt would say something about

One-Nine, and soon afterward there would be follow-ups, à la Admiral Boorda. They would tell the sad tale of Hugo Marder, the hero impostor, the men's clothing salesman who had posed as a war hero, who had worn another man's Silver Star lapel pin.

Hugo had one last dreadful thought as he entered the kitchen. Maybe this crazed chef would kill everybody. Not just him but everybody in the restaurant, including Melinda and Matt. That would also lead to Hugo's lie getting out and probably even making the papers.

He knew it was probably too late to change much of anything, but he did slip his right hand up to his lapel. He removed the Silver Star pin and stuck it in his coat pocket.

Other than death, Hugo had few ideas about what was waiting for Matt and him on the other side of that swinging kitchen door. He assumed there would be some kind of standoff with weapons and threats in progress, but it was also possible to find anything from corpses of dead people to chopped-up remains of dead bears.

He had already failed to move against the man with the pistol. What was it Robert had said in his story to Hugo about opportunity?

Here, no doubt, was another such opportunity coming up.

Except for the corpses, the scene in the kitchen turned out to be just about what he had imagined.

To the left stood You Johnny with a tiny silver pistol in his right hand. It was pointed at the back of the head of a man who was leaning on a tall white four-door refrigerator. The man had his hands extended above his head.

"You okay, Rick?" Matt said to the guy against the refrigerator.

"Not so good, to be honest, sir," said the man, clearly a Fish and Wildlife special agent who, among other things, was probably looking at his vanishing career in bear-part law enforcement. "I'm really sorry about this, sir, I really am."

"That's your automatic weapon the other guy has, isn't it?"

"Yes, sir, I'm sorry to report. Yes, sir. They distracted us, threw some hot soup on us, and he grabbed it. I'm really sorry about this."

Behind You Johnny were five or six young men in white work clothes, each sporting a knife or a hammer or some other kind of tool or cooking implement. Probably Thai kitchen helpers, prepared, al Qaeda–like, for mortal combat against the forces of the U.S. Fish and Wildlife Service. They were doing nothing at the moment but looking frightened out of their skins, staring at whatever moved, which was Matt and Hugo as they came in.

Straight ahead was a huge eight-burner cooking stove. A large stainless-steel pot was sitting on one of the lit gas burners. Steam and the now-familiar odor of bear claw soup were pouring up from the pot.

There was a tall dark man in a starched double-breasted white chef's outfit, complete with a high hat, standing defiantly in front of the stove. His arms were folded, and he held a bolo-size butcher knife in one hand, a long-handled stainless-steel ladle in the other.

To his left were at least a dozen men in blue or gray business suits — all of them mid-range-priced, off-the-rack — or SWAT-team outfits. There were traces of dark liquid on some of their clothes, and their faces seemed, to Hugo, red from embarrassment. They, too, if asked by Matt, no doubt would have confessed career-jeopardy sorrow for what had happened. The fact was that an old Thai man with a pistol, backed up by a chef and kitchen workers armed with cooking gear and hot soup, had neutralized a heavily armed federal anti-animal-parts strike force.

It might have been almost funny if not for the guy with the agent's machine gun. Hugo could feel his panting, anxious presence standing in front of the door into the restaurant.

Here now, ready or not, Hugo's moment had come.

You Johnny looked right at him — and only at him. He said, "A big mistake has been made by the agents of your government. We wish to begin some civilized talks with whoever is in charge so this matter can be resolved without further difficulty."

Hugo wanted to say something. He was expected to say something.

"We don't negotiate with terrorists," Matt barked defiantly, marinely. "It is against the policy of the United States government."

You Johnny turned his stare from Hugo to Matt. "We are not terrorists, sir. We own and operate this legally licensed restaurant here on Connecticut Avenue, Northwest, in your government's capital city."

"You stand there with a pistol pointed at the head of a duly sworn agent of the United States and claim you are no terrorist? Please!"

John Wayne's Sergeant Stryker himself

couldn't have said it better, thought Hugo. Oh, what silly ideas go through a man's mind at times of danger and stress!

"This firearm is also licensed, and I am employing it as a constructive tool of negotiation and reconciliation with the representatives of the government for which I have the utmost respect," said You Johnny.

"Pull the trigger and you will find out something about what our government respects," said Matt. War seemed near.

Hugo was struck with an idea — hopefully a Silver Star of an idea.

He walked directly to the chef in front of the stove. "May I take a look at the soup?" Hugo asked.

The chef smiled and lowered his guard and his weapons. "Certainly, certainly," he said. "An artist never minds having his work admired."

Hugo leaned over, again took in the pungent odor of something made from the cut-off claw of a bear, and pronounced, "Magnificent."

"Its magnificence is in its fragrance and taste," said the chef. "It has the power to improve your virility — your manhood."

You Johnny, from a few feet away, added, "That is what many Asian people believe. Mr. Jim Thompson and his friends in

Bangkok often partook. That is why we serve it here to a few of our friends on the anniversary of his disappearance. I had had some on several special occasions when I was a youngster because my father thought it would help me become a man. He told my mother that he was afraid that I was too womanlike and that bear claw soup's virility power might prevent me from becoming what he called a 'girl-boy.' That sensitive and ridiculous matter aside, what did happen was that I developed a real fondness for the taste of the special soup —"

"All right, enough of this!" yelled Matt. "Put the guns down, put your hands above your heads, and let's end this. Listen up as I give you your official warnings. Allow me to do so now: You — all of you — have the right to remain silent. But if you do choose to make a statement, it can and will be used against you in a court of law . . ."

Hugo was struck by the idea of giving an arrest warning to the people who were holding the guns at the moment. It was truly weird, bizarre — a joke. Maybe Matt was hoping that his audacious brazenness would cause them to give up their resistance? Hugo thought that unlikely.

Onward, Sir Hugo!

Ignoring Matt and his warning, Hugo

spoke again to the chef. "Would you mind demonstrating how you make this special soup?"

"Oh, sir, I would love to do that," said the chef.

As if on a stage, he eased his large ladle down into the bubbling soup, swished it around until he caught what he wanted, and raised something. It was a paw, complete with nails, about the size and shape of a deflated volleyball. The skin was dark brown. It was a terrible sight. Hugo considered the small spoonful of the soup that was down there in his stomach — or, more probable, now working its ugly mischief on his bloodstream and vital organs.

"You may wonder why it has no hair," said the happy chef, a man of forty or so who spoke with the trace of an accent that Hugo was not able to identify but assumed was Thai. The chef reached over to his left and picked up something that looked like gray clay.

"I began this process yesterday morning by washing this paw of a bear as clean as humanly possible and then wrapping it in this clay." The chef picked up a handful of the stuff and shoved it toward Hugo, who did not take any.

"Where did the paw come from?" Matt

demanded.

"I can answer that," said You Johnny. "It came from a private citizen in West Virginia, where the killing of the American brown bear is perfectly legal."

"Wrong, wrong — lie, lie," said Matt. "Our agents tracked it from a bear killed in a forest in northern Maine, where such action is illegal, and thus, under the federal law, it is illegal to transport or sell any part from it in interstate commerce. The bear was shot with a thirty-aught-six pump rifle at a range of a hundred yards. That paw — the right paw, and it was still warm, as was the rest of the dead bear — was severed from the carcass by persons — three white males — using a large hacksaw. We have videotape of the entire crime as it was being committed. We even have them on tape talking about getting the claw to Washington, to this restaurant, before Easter Sunday."

Hugo tried to imagine federal agents in camouflage gear, lurking about a Maine forest, videotaping the dismembering of a brown bear.

The chef ignored Matt and You Johnny and said loudly to Hugo, "Continuing the process, sir, I then placed the clay-wrapped paw in our oven and cooked it at a 375-degree temperature for three hours. When I took it out of the oven, I removed the clay packing, leaving the paw tender — and hairless."

He picked up the paw and shoved it toward Hugo, who smiled graciously but declined to take the dead brown bear's paw. I'm not ready for this, either!

The master chef kept the paw in his right hand as a kind of prop. "Now the real art began. This afternoon I put the paw in this pot, which was full of simmering water. After an hour, I began to add the final ingredients. Some sherry, some salt and black pepper, some green chilies, a few strips of red peppers, dashes of curry and cumin, two cups of raisins, some freshly crushed tomatoes, as well as a few shreds of lean ham and chicken. The simmering continued for another couple of hours, at which time I took a first taste, added some more seasoning ingredients, and left it on low heat until this evening. The end product was what went to a few select patrons tonight. Were you one of them?"

"I was indeed." Hugo clapped his hands. Nobody else joined in. But the chef gave a polite bow. As he had said, he was an artist in need of appreciation.

Hugo could tell from Matt's body language that he was out of patience. He said,

"No more PBS cooking-school demonstrations, no more of anything except handing over weapons, freeing hostages, and ending this thing before somebody gets hurt."

"Here's what's going to happen," said Hugo with a forcefulness that startled everyone, including Hugo. "Matt here will replace the agent at the refrigerator as your hostage, You Johnny. You will keep your pistol, but your man with the machine gun will lay it down and leave the kitchen, as will everyone else on both sides."

"I said no negotiations!" Matt yelled.

"You Johnny and I will do the negotiating," Hugo said. "You, Special Agent Matthew Columbia, will only witness."

It was the moment of truth — *a* moment of truth.

Hugo Colin Marder, still only a clothing salesman not ready to be a former marine, was playing out something that was over his head. But he was under the power of something Emily's politicians called momentum. He had been forced to act this way by that little lapel pin.

Matt gave Hugo a look that said, *Who in the hell do you think you are, clothing salesman?* But, after two or three beats, he said, "Okay. But this better be good."

"Semper Fi," Hugo said.

Matt only frowned.

Hugo looked at You Johnny. "What about it?"

You Johnny moved away from his agent prisoner, motioned to the man with the machine gun, and said to Hugo, "I am willing to put my fate in your hands."

Within a few seconds, it was just the three of them — Hugo, Matt, and You Johnny — in the kitchen. The last words spoken by the departing others came from the chef: "Any of you, all of you, please help yourself to some soup if you like."

Hugo suggested to You Johnny and Matt that they all sit down around a small table over in the corner of the kitchen. Small stacks of bills and notes and credit-card receipts, plus an electric calculator, a telephone, and a white plastic radio were on the table.

You Johnny proposed they take the chef's offer and each grab a bowl of the bear claw soup on the way. "It will be good for the spirits of peace and compromise," he said.

"I cannot and will not consume something that could be evidence in a criminal case," said Matt. "Besides that, I hear it tastes like warmed-over mud."

Hugo also took a pass on more soup.

He had no idea what he was going to do next. He would just try to make a sale, to both of them at the same time. A sale of some sense, not of clothes.

After they were seated, he asked You Johnny to give his side of the story.

"I swear that the man I dealt with said the bear paw was coming from West Virginia, where such things are legal. He lied to me, if it really came from Maine, and that would make me a victim of the crime, not part of it."

"That's true, isn't it?" Hugo asked Matt.

"Will you help us nail the guy?" Matt asked You Johnny.

"Nail, sir?"

"Identify him, testify against him."

"Do I have a choice?"

"Sure. You can stiff us and go to prison for resisting arrest, holding a loaded firearm on a federal agent. Sure, you don't have to help us."

"The man was sitting in the restaurant when all of this began," said You Johnny. "In fact, he was at the table next to yours. He's a citizen of Thailand who buys animal parts here and sells them to exclusive restaurants and to wealthy citizens in our country and in Japan and Singapore."

"The guy who grabbed Melinda?" Hugo

asked Matt.

"Most probably, yes. It makes sense. He must have realized that he was about to have one very serious problem. That means we've got him — great." Then, to You Johnny, he said, "Do we have a deal?"

As if dealing with a tailor on a fitting for a new suit, Hugo said, "In exchange, Mr. You Johnny would require that no criminal charges be filed against him or any of his employees for anything that happened here tonight."

"True, oh, yes, true, please," said You Johnny.

"I can't let the guy who grabbed the automatic weapon off the hook," Matt said.

"He's my assistant chef, and he's my grandson — an impressionable young man only rising to the defense of his grandfather."

"Come on, Matt," Hugo said. "He didn't hurt anything but some windows in his own family's restaurant."

Matt frowned, then smiled, and they all shook hands. Hugo had made the sale.

"I now must make a confession," said You Johnny. "My pistol is not loaded, as was frequently alleged, and it never has been. I keep it around for effect, not for use."

Matt shook his head. "My last case before

this involved the illegal smuggling of sturgeon from the Caspian Sea through JFK Airport in New York. The one before that had to do with exotic birds coming into Miami from South America. They were nothing compared to this goddamn stupid fucking thing."

Matt Columbia is definitely a former marine, thought Hugo.

Outside a short time later, after saying goodbye to Melinda and the others, Hugo stuck the Silver Star pin back into his coat lapel. Before he could start his walk back to his house, he felt a heavy hand on his shoulder. He turned to see Matt.

"I owe you an apology, Hugo," he said. Then, pointing at the Silver Star pin in Hugo's lapel, he added, "I have to confess, I had some doubts about that and you being a marine."

Hugo was not able to speak.

Matt was. "You didn't look like a marine to me at the beginning. The way you walked and carried yourself . . . bearing, presence. That's what it's called in the Corps, as you know. You didn't have any of that. And you didn't react too well when that guy first pulled a gun."

Hugo braced for the worst. Was Matt going to throw him against a wall, handcuff him, and read him his rights?

"But I knew I was wrong in that kitchen," Matt said. "Marines move out. You moved out. Nobody got hurt, thanks to you. You're not only a good marine, you're a damned fine salesman. It takes all kinds."

Matt turned toward the restaurant and then back to Hugo. "Semper Fi, Hugo."

"Semper Fi, Matt."

Matt went quickly back to the restaurant.

Hugo did an about-face and headed even more quickly toward his red door and his new being as a former marine.

As he moved out, he thought he heard the sound of a band playing a marine kind of marching song.

# FOUR

*The Marine Officer's Guide* arrived on Tuesday.

There, on page 313, under the boldface heading "Your Military Occupational Specialty (MOS)," Hugo read:

When you report to Basic School, you are classified as a basic officer. You retain this classification only until basic training is completed and the Marine Corps has had an opportunity to size you up. Before you leave Basic School, you are assigned a primary MOS by the Commandant of the Marine Corps as a basic officer in one of the following major fields of command specialization:

*Infantry:* Occupational field 03

*Antiaircraft artillery:* Occupational field 07

*Field artillery:* Occupational field 08

And so on, through Engineer, Armor/amphibian tractor, Communications, Motor Transport, and others.

Hugo now knew what an MOS was.

Over the next several evenings, he worked at his computer and with a pen and a yellow legal pad to plan his transformation into a former marine.

He created major headings, then added notes and lists under each.

— Physical appearance: hair, body (lose weight)

—Walk. Like a marine (get video of marines marching)

— What Matt called "bearing, presence" (must be videos of that)

— Talk. Like a marine. Learn lingo. From movies? Officers Guide? (learn how to say "fuck" naturally?)

— My marine experience. Invent complete story from beginning to end
 When joined?
 Serial number?
 *MOS!*
 Where trained?

Outfit in Vietnam (One-Nine? yes! the Walking Dead)

Battles in Vietnam (every one I was in)

How won Silver Star

Details of exactly what happened . . . or not (maybe just refuse to talk about it? Like Zorba's Navy Cross marine?)

— Mementoes of my service. Buy off Internet

Uniforms (dress blues? why not?)

Emblems

Equipment

Souvenirs

— Learn marine history: basics with some knowledge of famous battles of World Wars I and II, and Korea, as well as Vietnam

— Study up on famous marine heroes: real ones, like Basilone

— Memorize all verses of Marine Hymn and other marine customs and procedures

— Buy some marine stuff: T-shirts, baseball caps, desk sets, more cuff links, etc.

There was eBay for auctions, but, through Google, he found several other websites for acquiring the knowledge and purchasing some of the items he would need for the transformation.

Hugo had no idea how long it would take to become a former marine, one capable of passing the serious scrutiny of the Matts of the marine world who might come along. But he was convinced he could pull it off.

He also had no idea where that confidence was coming from.

Could it be that just wearing the Silver Star of a man from the Walking Dead had done this?

The first videotape to arrive was called *The Making of a Marine,* a painfully detailed account in full color with grunting sounds of marine boot camp at the Parris Island and San Diego recruit depots.

Hugo felt the most agony watching the shaved-head recruits endure the Crucible, a fifty-four-hour marathon of physical and mental testing at the end of boot camp. Wearing full combat gear and carrying metal ammunition boxes, they hiked a total of forty miles while, along the way, mastering such "events" as an enemy-mined rope bridge, ferocious pugil stick encounters, and pop-up assaults by guerrillas. When they finally staggered back to base camp, they were assembled around a small replica of the Iwo Jima statue, handed eagle and globe marine emblems for their uniforms, and told they could now call themselves marines.

Hugo saw what lay ahead as his own version of the Crucible.

The body.

That definitely had to be one of the reasons Matt, the bear claw cop, had not seen Hugo as a marine. It wasn't exactly because Hugo was fat and out of shape, but more that his weight didn't quite fit the shape in the right places.

He was five-eleven and weighed 178 pounds. His build was rather slight at the top, in his shoulders, neck, and arms, while rather full in his midsection, rear, and legs. To suggest that he resembled a Coke bottle — as an idiot trainer at a Washington health club once had, would be unfair and inaccurate. To say, as Emily often had, that he sometimes appeared "top-light and bottom-heavy" was also unfair but, regrettably, mostly accurate.

Whatever, he knew he had his work cut out for him to transform his body into that of a marine. Much of what he was now physically was permanent, so he knew that it was probably impossible to alter much. But he had to give it a try. If he was going to *be* a former marine, he had to look like one.

*Semper Fit — The Marine Corps Workout* was where he began. It was a video of real marine drill instructors at the San Diego recruit depot taking a group of sweating, miserable real marine boots through thirty-five minutes of calisthenics hell.

Hugo, who got up each morning at seven-thirty, reset his alarm for six-thirty. He immediately slipped into a pair of khaki marine-issue shorts and T-shirt — bought from a military equipment website — trotted into his den, clicked on the TV and VCR, and exercised with the marines.

The first morning he could barely get through the five-minute warm-up and stretching moves, which involved relatively simple things like twisting both arms, one at a time, behind his head and leaning forward on his outstretched legs, one at a time.

But over the next few days, Hugo began tackling the "daily nine," some of which, such as pumping iron and pull-ups, he simply ignored for equipment reasons. But he did push-ups, including some called "dive-bombers," as well as stomach crunches, side-straddle hops, back extensions, and sit-ups, among other atrocities.

He did the marines' stair-step run up and down the first two steps of the stairway to his second floor.

He did all of this while making the same cadence noises of the marines.

Ooo Rah,
Oh, Yah,
Lefty right,
Lef rah . . .

Hugo also went on a diet for the first time in his life. After several informational browses on the Internet, he settled on the South Beach Diet. The consensus was that it was the simplest, quickest, and easiest of the new low-carb diets.

The diet was simple, all right. For the first two weeks, no sweets, bread, fruits (not even orange juice!), potatoes, rice, or booze, among other delicious things. But that did leave high-protein food such as beef, chicken, veal, cheese, and even unsalted nuts, and most vegetables except corn.

It said nothing, one way or another, about bear claw soup.

The walk.

Since he had taken his first steps in Michigan, Hugo sprang off the balls of his feet rather than stepped. His heels seldom touched the ground, said his parents and the director of the high school marching band, for which Hugo played successfully but marched unsuccessfully as a bass drummer. The spring was still there in every step. In Emily's words, "I can see you coming a mile away through a crowd because your head is always popping up and down like a bouncing ball."

From the Marine Corps Heritage Foundation's website, Hugo bought a VHS tape of marching marines, including boot camp recruits as well as others in polished ceremonies at the Marine Barracks in Washington and in parades up Pennsylvania Avenue and other notable places.

There were no bouncers here. Whether drill-team marines or boots, they all moved their legs forward with an apparent effortlessness, barely raising their feet off the ground and ending each step heel-down. Their backs were straight, their shoulders back, their heads erect.

Hugo began in front of his hallway mirror. It took an amazingly short period of time — less than a couple of hours — for him to eliminate the bounce. It made him wonder why in the hell he hadn't done this years ago.

His daily walk to and from work, half an hour each way, helped him solidify and make more or less permanent his new marine way to walk, to carry himself.

Mama mama can't you see,
What the Marines have done for me,
I used to drive a Cadillac
Now I'm humping with a pack . . .
Oh Leh ooo Leh,
Oh Leh ooo,
Oh Leh ooo leh . . .

He called such cadences to himself, being careful not to do it so loudly that it would scare his fellow pedestrians coming and going between Dupont Circle and downtown Washington. One cadence, about doing something with the very cold body part of an Eskimo woman, he was particularly anxious for no one to hear.

Soon his toes were always pointed straight ahead while he walked, automatically squaring his corners and turns in a military manner. And when he stopped, he brought his feet together and then extended them as he clasped his hands behind his back in the parade-rest position.

Sometimes his marching and pausing style drew puzzled stares or smiles. Hugo enjoyed the attention and often smiled back.

One morning a well-dressed young man, possibly on his way to a K Street legal office, did more than one double take when he stopped next to Hugo at a red light. "Hard to get it out of the system, isn't it?" Hugo said.

*Isn't it?* From the startled look on the guy's face, Hugo read the answer: *I have no idea what you're talking about, old man.*

Hugo figured there was not even anything as military as a John Wayne or Van Heflin movie in this kid's life experience.

As Emily had constantly reminded him, politics was not his forte. But it occurred to him that morning that the politicians of America should wake up to the fact that a majority of Americans today knew little or nothing about the lives of the young people they sent off to fight wars.

He assumed, though, that the president and all of his people who were taking the country to war against Iraq knew about those kids. Hugo knew for sure that the one thing this country did not need was another Vietnam.

He mumbled something to himself about how important it was to stop that fool Saddam Hussein from using his stockpiles of nuclear, chemical, and biological weapons against us.

He could hardly wait to see the pictures of all those weapons once the war was over.

The talk.

Hugo knew from the movies that talking like a marine might mean using the F-word not only as a verb but also as an adjective, adverb, and every other part of speech.

But Hugo had never been a foul mouth. There was no moral or other reason except that of environment. His father seldom had said anything stronger than "hell" or "damn," his mother never even went that far, and few others, including the jocks, in high school or at Michigan Western State, had, either. Profanity, scatological and otherwise, was simply absent from his early life.

Emily changed that for a while. She, like him, had picked up nothing in Michigan, but working in the Washington office of a congressman — even one from Michigan — had exposed her to a world where telling people they were full of shit was considered routinely edgy and/or cute. As Emily explained, "Politics is combat, so the language of combat is appropriate." Toward the end of their time together, she seldom spoke a dozen sentences before inserting at least a "crap" or a "piss" if not a "shit" or — on very rare occasions — a "fuck." "Asshole" was her absolute favorite. Most everyone she came across who wasn't a Republican — a moderate Michigan Gerald Ford kind of Republican — was an asshole. That meant there were a lot of assholes in her daily labors as a legislative assistant in a Congress where conservative Republicans and Democrats of all kinds combined to form an overwhelming majority.

Interestingly enough, Hugo's almost exclusively male environment at Nash Brothers was nearly as word-clean as small-town Michigan had been. Few if any of the sales associates really cussed beyond a stray bad word about a particularly difficult customer. Hugo had never heard either Robert or Jackson swear. Hugo did hear some foul stuff from the occasional customer, some of whom, now that he thought about it, may have been former marines.

The derivatives of "fuck" aside, Hugo knew that if he was going to walk the Marine Walk, he would also have to talk the Marine Talk.

So. He tore the glossary out of *The Marine Officer's Guide* and began carrying it with him, referring to it and memorizing various terms when he had breaks during his day.

He learned, among other things, that marines' beds were racks, their ceilings were overheads, their candy was pogey-bait, their bars were slopshutes, their big eaters were chowhounds, and their neckties were field scarves.

There was nothing in the guide about the tone and manner in which these and all other words should actually be delivered, so Hugo rented *Sands of Iwo Jima* and *Battle Cry.* He figured there could be no better Marine Talk role models than John Wayne and Van Heflin.

Meanwhile, he began slowly working on a comfort level with the F-word. Ease with using it as an imperative verb came the quickest. He became particularly relaxed with "Fuck you!" after only a few quiet practice tries into the front hall mirror.

The story. The *phony* story.

It took three weeks of browsing through and absorbing information before Hugo felt he was prepared to create the detailed narrative of Hugo Marder, USMC.

The best way to do it, he concluded, was to simply write it down in the form of a brief sketch of his marine service.

He would use first person. He would say it like he would if he were telling his story to someone in person. He would write it like he would talk it.

He started in longhand, writing in ball-point pen on a yellow legal pad, but after a few sentences, he switched to his computer. He was a pretty fair typist, and he thought it might go faster. If nothing else, it would look better and more real, more official. But it still came slowly and with difficulty, reminding him that he was a men's clothing salesman, not a writer. He hadn't written anything more than notes and a few letters since school, but he figured it really didn't matter that much now. He was only doing this for himself, as a way to implant into his own memory and soul his life — his *fraudulent* life — as a U.S. Marine.

He began with just about the only tiny pieces of information that were true.

I wanted to be a U.S. Marine since my boyhood in Michigan. The Vietnam War was on when I graduated from high school and I thought of acting then on my child-hood dream and enlisting in the marines. But then I thought about it some more and concluded that it would be best to get a college degree first. That was important for my family and would be important for me later in life. I thought, too, that with a college degree I could still be a marine, but, possibly, if I was qualified and had the right stuff, I could be a commissioned officer.

So I went to college at Michigan Western State College in Kalamazoo, majoring in business administration with a minor in art, which got me an automatic deferment from the draft. In my sophomore year my desire to be a marine hardened (crystallized?). I went to the office of the Naval ROTC on campus and learned that I could sign up for a marine officer program called the Platoon Leaders Class — PLC. I would go to training in Quantico, Virginia, during the coming summer and again the next one between my junior and senior year. Then, on the day I graduated, I would be commissioned a second lieutenant and report immediately to Basic School, also at Quantico. (Basic School's purpose, according to the guide, was "to train newly commissioned lieutenants in the duties and responsibilities of Marine officers, ashore and afloat, with emphasis on the duties of an infantry platoon leader.")

That's what I did. The summers were tough. So was Basic School. But it was worth it to be a marine.

When I left Basic School after six

months, I was given an 03 MOS — infantry. I was given orders to report to Okinawa, where I was assigned to the First Battalion, Ninth Marines. That is in the Third Marine Division, which had many units in Vietnam. I knew that it would be dangerous, particularly for me. They told us repeatedly in Basic School that the life expectancy in combat of a marine second lieutenant platoon leader was around twenty-eight seconds.

I was awarded the Silver Star, but it is not false modesty for me to say that I don't want to talk about it. I am proud of the honor and my medal — that's why I wear the lapel pin. Talking about it, though, seems egoistic, for one thing, and brings back too many bad memories, for another. Suffice to say that my platoon was attacked by a large force of Vietcong in some high grass in A Shau Valley during what was called Operation Dewey Canyon. Several of my men were hit. I went to the rescue of one while under fire and protected him with my body until he could be rescued. That's why they gave me the Silver Star. There were many more deserving marines in our outfit and others who did truly heroic things for which they either received or deserved to receive the Silver

Star or even something higher. That's all I want to say about it. Was I wounded? Only slightly. Nothing serious. I was awarded the Purple Heart but I don't think I deserved that, either, frankly. It was just a scratch on my left leg that didn't even leave a permanent scar. I was also promoted to first lieutenant and made executive officer of B Company in One-Nine.

I returned to the States in July 1969 and left the Marine Corps shortly thereafter. I had served three years, four months, two weeks, and three days on active duty. My serial number was 081278.

One-Nine suffered staggering losses in my battle and others in Vietnam. So many were killed and wounded it was given the nickname "the Walking Dead." As a unit, it was deactivated in 1998.

I am proud to have served in the U.S. Marine Corps and with the Walking Dead of One-Nine.

Lies, lies, lies. And more lies.

There wasn't an NROTC program at Michigan Western. Hugo had not been a war protester, but he simply hadn't been interested in fighting in a war. The marine dream had never seriously resurfaced. All of his friends had felt the same way about the war, even if they'd kept it mostly to themselves. The tradition in their hometowns, as in Hugo's, was to go to war — to serve. But there had been no heat from family or friends back home to do it this time. Most everyone Hugo knew had turned away from it as an issue. No judgments were openly expressed one way or the other. Nobody wanted anyone's child or grandchild to go to Vietnam, but nobody wanted there to be any antiwar odor to that belief, either.

They wanted it both ways, and for the most part, they got what they wanted.

The hair.

There wasn't enough hair left on the top of Hugo's head to do a full-fledged crew cut, marine-style. But, inspired by the various videotapes he'd watched of real marines, he went one better.

"You're kidding, Mr. Marder," said his barber, Angelo Boone. "You don't really want me to remove every bit of hair you have?"

"I'm not kidding. Shave it bald!"

Angelo used a heavy-duty electric shaver and, for some final work, a straight razor and shaving lotion to remove from Hugo's head every sign of his graying dark blond hair.

When it was over, Angelo twirled the barber chair around so Hugo could see himself in the large panoramic mirror that covered the wall behind.

"Oh my God!" Hugo said in mock horror. "Put it back on, Angelo — all of it!"

Angelo, a man in his sixties who had been cutting Hugo's hair for nearly twelve years, pointed to the scraps and tufts of Hugo's hair that surrounded the base of the chair. "Help yourself, sir. You pick it up, and I'll go get some airplane glue."

Hugo smiled and stood. "You did a perfect job, Angelo." He handed his barber thirty dollars.

"Perfect, if you want to be Yul Brynner in the movies or you want to be a pirate or a wrestler or a marine — something like that," said Angelo.

"Something like that is precisely what I want to be," said Hugo, which only confused Angelo.

While Hugo had already become a devoted believer in the supreme informational power of the Internet, his shaved head came as a solid confirmation.

Before his trip to the barber, Hugo had visited the limitless glories of Google. A straightforward "shaved head" search brought up the website headshaverman

.com. From the time Hugo left Angelo's chair, he followed the maintenance procedures recommended on the site.

It meant setting his alarm clock back another fifteen minutes, because he had to completely shave his head with a Gillette Mach3 razor and Edge ProGel while showering each morning. "Always shave wet," said the omniscent adviser. "The hair is softer and easier to remove. Never use shaving cream, because it makes it too hard to see what you're doing. Change blades on the razor after every second or third shave."

The website also had a series of questions and answers with the man in charge. One of the more interesting sets:

Q: What's the proper term for a person with a shaved head?

A: I'm not aware of a proper term. Terms that I've heard include: bald, bald-by-choice, shaved, smooth, hairless, skinhead, Mr. Clean, cue-balled, and smooth-skulled. Other terms exist; use what you are most comfortable with. Note, however, that "skinhead" properly refers to a subculture that got its start as a working-class movement in England in the 1960s and is not really appropriate for the majority of people with shaved heads. "Bald" is probably the most proper term for anyone without hair.

Hugo's weight loss and new ways of walking and talking had not gone unnoticed at the store, but for the most part, everyone accepted Hugo's general explanation: "I've decided to reshape myself in more ways than one."

But showing up bald was a major event — an escalation.

Before opening, Jackson Dyer was the first to see Hugo.

"Fall asleep in the barber chair, Hugo?" he quipped.

"Got your head caught in a blender, Hugo?" said one of the sales associates.

"Stay out of the sunlight with that head," said another. "The reflection will blind everyone around you."

Only Robert got it, of course. Hugo had told him of his ultimate intentions and had kept him posted on his progress. "What is that marines say — Semper Paralysis?" he said now to Hugo.

"Semper *Fidelis,* which means 'Always Faithful,' " said Hugo, laughing. "Semper Fi, for short."

"All right, then — Semper Fi, Sir Hugo." Robert gave Hugo a kind of salute, raising two fingers of his right hand to his forehead.

Hugo resisted the urge to tell Robert that nobody but a marine was allowed to use the greeting.

Robert looked at Hugo's waist. "Down, down, you're going. Do you have a goal — a grail?"

"Thirty-two and a half," Hugo said with pride.

"From what?"

"Thirty-five and a half."

"Semper Fi doubled, Sir Hugo," Robert said.

The next morning Hugo called Jackson Dyer just before eight-forty-five. That was when Jackson always left his home in suburban northern Virginia.

"There's some congestion in the chest — nothing serious, I'm sure," Hugo said in a faked semi-laryngitis voice.

"Spend the day getting well, Hugo," Jackson said. "God knows you've got plenty of sick days coming to you."

What God also knew was that it was all a lie. Hugo stayed home so he could watch *Something for the Birds* on the FOX Movie Channel at 10:10 A.M.

Since taping programs off the television with his VCR was a skill he had yet to master effectively, he had to watch the eighty-one-minute movie either this morning or tonight, beginning at three minutes after midnight, which was too late.

So, only two weeks after showing up at the store past opening, here he was, also for the first time in his seventeen years at Nash Brothers, lying about being sick.

*Something for the Birds,* it turned out, was mostly a Washington love story between lobbyist Steve Bennett (Victor Mature) and do-gooder Anne Richards (Patricia Neal). But Hugo's sole interest was in Johnnie Adams, a little old man played by Edmund Gwenn who is called Admiral at the many fancy Washington parties he attends, wearing a Navy Cross lapel pin in his suit coat. At one such party, Johnnie meets Richards, who has come from California to block legislation that would destroy a bird sanctuary. Johnnie, clearly a good man in every respect, agrees to help her.

A villainous corporate executive on the other side of the issue says of Johnnie Adams, "Anybody that honest must have something to hide."

"I'm no hero," Johnnie tells Richards after saying he wants out of the lobbying fight, following the threat of exposure of what, in fact, he does have to hide.

"A man who won a Navy Cross doesn't quit under fire," Richards replies.

But, of course, he didn't win the Navy Cross, and he isn't any kind of admiral. Johnnie's an engraver at a print shop who helps himself to invitations to parties, where he regularly eats and drinks well and strikes up acquaintances with the socially powerful of Washington.

Johnnie resists the blackmail and is publicly unmasked as a fraud. But it turns out just fine, because the Navy Cross was won by Johnnie's dead hero son in World War I. And Johnnie hangs in there with Richards, now in love with Bennett, who also helps to successfully kill the anti-bird legislation.

Johnnie, pointing to the Navy Cross lapel pin, tells a Senate committee, "Wearing this pin made quitting and running hard to do."

End of Johnnie Adams's story.

Hugo could only hope that his own would have such a pleasant conclusion.

# FIVE

He was ready.

His waistline was marine. So were his walk and his talk. And now his head was as ready on the inside as it was on the outside.

Hugo now knew that the Marine Corps mission words were Honor, Courage, and Commitment. He knew that the Corps had been founded in 1775 by the Continental Congress as the first military force of what was to become the United States of America. The first marines were recruited at a tavern in Philadelphia — Tun Tavern, it was called — to go aboard colonial ships. He learned about the battles of Belleau Wood during World War I and about the Pacific Island landings — Tarawa, Saipan, Peleliu, Guadalcanal, and Iwo Jima — in World War II, where it was said "uncommon valor was a common virtue." And there were the Inchon landing and the Chosin Reservoir of the Korean War and the many marine operations during the Vietnam War, including his "own" with One-Nine.

He knew: "First to fight" had been the marines' cry almost from the beginning. After Belleau Wood, the Germans called the marines "Devil Dogs," a term that stuck. So did "Leathernecks," which came from their early shipboard days of wearing leather around their necks to protect against sword slashes. The red stripe down the trousers of the dress blue uniform stood for the blood shed by marines. Marines never left their dead or wounded on the battlefield. Marines went through the roughest recruit training of any military organization in the world. Marines believed they were only as strong and as safe as the men on either side of them.

Hugo had watched *Battle Cry* twice and *Sands of Iwo Jima* once. He had read about real marine heroes, including John Basilone from the boyhood comic book but also Smedley Butler, Chesty Puller, Joe Foss, and Pappy Boyington, among many others. He went over lists of now-famous former marines — Secretaries of State Shultz and Baker, John Glenn, Art Buchwald, Mark Russell, Jonathan Winters, Don Imus, Mark Shields, Ted Williams, Jerry Coleman, Lee Trevino, Steve McQueen, Gene Hackman,

George C. Scott, Frederick Lane and both Hugh Brannum and Bob Keeshan, better known as Mr. Green Jeans and Captain Kangaroo of children's TV fame. Hugo put out of his mind that people such as Lee Harvey Oswald and Charles Whitman, the Texas tower sniper, had also been marines.

Hugh had also watched the *Pageantry of the Corps* tape, featuring the routinely spectacular performances of the Marine Band, the Marine Drum and Bugle Corps, and the precision drill teams at the Eighth and Eye Marine Barracks in Washington. He had baseball caps, desk sets, T-shirts, and sweats emblazoned with marine emblems and sayings. For the last four weeks, he had worn none of his cuff links except the new marines pair. He had also replaced his regular white underwear with marine-issue olive-brown skivvies he had bought from a marine website.

In his closet now hung a marine officer's dress blue uniform, as well as one green (winter service) and one tan (summer service), complete with first lieutenant's bars and appropriate caps and hats. Over the left chest of the dress uniform hung the Silver Star. The ribbon was on the greens. All items had been purchased in eBay auctions. He had no intention of ever wearing the uniforms in public. They were to be part of his spiritual preparation.

How could he know how it felt to be a U.S. Marine without ever having worn the uniform?

Now it was Saturday. *The* Saturday for what he had come to see as his own kind of Crucible. The time had come to test himself. A symposium at the Smithsonian Institution would be his battlefield.

He took the uniforms from the closet, the dress blues first. The dark tunic and light trousers fit and felt good. He placed the white cap on his head and went to the full-length mirror in the hallway.

He liked the man he saw.

He went back to his bedroom, changed into the dress green uniform, and returned to the mirror.

Yes. *I am a marine.*

Then he changed into a dark blue hop-sack blazer, a pair of gray flannel slacks, a button-down blue oxford dress shirt, and a solid wine-colored silk tie.

This would be his uniform on this important day.

He put the Silver Star pin in the lapel of the blazer. His right hand shook slightly when he held the lapel pin. It took a few more seconds to get it through the hole than it had before.

Twenty minutes later, there was some vibration through his entire body as he entered the Smithsonian Building, one of several on the south side of National Mall next to the original redbrick Castle structure.

He was there for a Smithsonian Semper Fidelis seminar, an open-to-the-public event Hugo had discovered in his Internet wanderings. He had reserved a seat through the Smithsonian website. The Commandant of the Marine Corps had spoken on Friday night, and today, Saturday afternoon at three, there was to be a discussion called "Celebrating the Corps."

Hugo arrived via the Metro — Dupont Circle Station to Smithsonian Station — nearly a half hour early so he could observe the audience and scene. If he didn't like what he saw, he could, in marine jargon, bug out.

Give up his attempt at a Second Coming as a former marine.

Hugo stood in the auditorium foyer and watched as people, most of them men, showed their tickets to attendants and streamed on into the auditorium. There was another door out of his range of sight, so he wasn't able to see everyone. But of the ones he could, more than half were fifty or older, although there were a few in their twenties and thirties. All were clearly marines, past or present it seemed to Hugo; almost to a man, they walked with their head up and chest back and had a close haircut. The young ones mostly had shaved sideburns, and some, like Hugo, had no hair at all.

Though Hugo had prepared for the possibility of a former marine See You, there were none among those he saw.

With five minutes to go, he sucked it in, said "Move out!" to himself, and went into the auditorium. The man who took his ticket spotted the Silver Star pin and said, "Good afternoon — and Semper Fi, Marine."

"Semper Fi," Hugo responded.

Inside, the arrangement was that of a small theater, some two hundred or so cushioned seats facing a stage, where the panelists sat. They were three prominent former marines — two funny men, the newspaper columnist Art Buchwald and the satirist Mark Russell, plus one unfunny one, the TV network anchor Frederick Lane. The moderator was an ex–*Washington Herald* reporter and editor named James Dickenson, also a former marine.

Hugo found a seat in the last row and perused the crowd, mostly from the back. He recognized no one. He had come prepared for several possible run-in difficulties. That was part of the testing — the Crucible.

Dickenson was a balding man in his sixties with the build of a football linebacker and the forceful manner and voice of a marine. He began with introductions that were a mix of funny and serious. They included a line or two about the panelists' marine service, barely three years in each case. Lane had been an infantry officer in the Second Marine Division in the mid-fifties. Buchwald and Russell had served in aviation units as enlisted men — Russell also in the fifties, Buchwald during World War II.

Hugo was delighted to see that Dickenson was the only person on the stage who would have been picked out of a lineup as a former marine. Lane and Russell were nothing very impressive physically, both about Hugo's size and build. Buchwald, short and paunchy, was even more — or less — so.

Dickenson started by asking each why he had joined the marines. Russell said he did it to avoid the draft, after being inspired by watching the old marine movie *What Price Glory,* starring James Cagney and Dan Dailey. Buchwald, only seventeen, had enlisted to escape high school and to impress a woman named Flossie Starling in Greensboro, North Carolina, who ended up rejecting him for a Virginia Military Institute cadet.

Lane said that for him, going into the marines had been automatic, because both his father and older brother had been marines before him.

"I had dreamed of being a marine since I was a little boy," he said.

*Me, too!* Hugo wanted to shout. But he didn't.

Within minutes, Russell confirmed beyond any doubt that this was a gathering of marines, foul mouths and all.

"I was an enlisted man. We no longer had the Japanese or even the North Koreans to hate, so we hated our officers. They were much more sophisticated than us. They had gone to college. They knew which fork to use. They knew exactly what wine to serve with shit on a shingle."

Hugo had no idea what *that* was. But from the laughter, two things were clear — this room was full of former marines, and they definitely knew about shit on a shingle. Hugo thought that there must be few other public events in Washington where the word "shit" was used in the first few minutes and was warmly and naturally received.

Russell brought down the house, and for the next hour, it stayed mostly down with his and Buchwald's stories and quips, all delivered in different New York accents. Buchwald was from Queens, Russell from Buffalo.

Buchwald said, "It's no secret that there weren't many Jews in the Marine Corps back then. In my unit of four hundred marines, I was the only one. The other marines were always picking fights with me. I thought it was because I was a Jew, and I always fought back to defend my faith. But then I realized they weren't fighting me because I was a Jew. It was because I was an asshole."

Russell said, "I don't know what it's like now, but the peacetime Corps of the fifties was guided by one driving obsession — good grooming. Thinking my days would be filled with weaponry and dangerous maneuvers, I enlisted only to spend my three years qualifying with Blitz cloth, brass polish, shoe polish, floor wax, and starch. Instead of coming home as John Wayne, I returned as Martha Stewart."

Buchwald told the story of going to the

Gridiron Show, a white-tie dinner where the president and the rest of the Washington elite socialized. The Marine Band played a brief concert and ended with the song from each of the armed services.

"When they played the song of each service, everyone in the room who served in it was supposed to stand," said Buchwald. "When they played the Marine Hymn, I stood. I heard a guy across the table say to the guy next to him, 'Why is Buchwald standing up?' The other guy said, 'He was a marine.' And the other guy said, 'Jesus Christ!' "

Lane told a story about his father, who enlisted in the marines when he was seventeen because he saw a sign in a recruiting station window that said LEARN TO FLY — JOIN THE MARINES.

"He enlisted, served four years in the infantry, mostly in Haiti, and never laid eyes on an airplane — much less learned how to fly one."

Buchwald said he was upset when he was assigned to aviation ordnance rather than to the infantry at the end of boot camp on Parris Island.

"I went to my D.I., and I said, 'My recruiting sergeant said I could be a paratrooper.' The D.I. said, 'Okay, you're a paratrooper.' "

Russell said the only time he was in danger was when "I let my sideburns grow one half inch lower than the top of my ears." That was against regulations, and he was given a one-week restriction.

Lane spoke mostly about how being a marine platoon leader had forced him to grow up fast, pushing him to his physical and mental limits, and making it possible for him since to relax about proving how tough he was on television or anywhere else. "I did that in the marines." He also went on and on — too long, it seemed to Hugo — about how his marine experience had turned him into an advocate of mandatory national service.

Buchwald's serious stuff was about how the Marine Corps, most particularly his D.I. and the ten weeks he spent at Parris Island, turned him, "a messed-up kid," into a man. An orphan, he said the marines had become his father.

Russell and the others spoke about the special status conferred on them from having been marines, and the immediate bond that is ignited when two former marines meet for the first time.

"Whatever we did or didn't do while in the Corps, or whatever lies we tell about it, we're all proud we're marines," said Russell.

When it was over, the crowd gave them a standing ovation. Dickenson, who apparently moderated a lot of Smithsonian events, said it was the first time that had happened. Marines cheering other marines? It seemed like a natural thing to Hugo, who clapped and cheered as loudly as anyone in the room.

He felt at home and strangely comfortable, considering the riskiest part of his Saturday-afternoon Crucible was still to come.

That was the reception. Coffee and cookies in the auditorium lobby with Buchwald, Russell, and Lane and the other members of the audience.

Onward? Yes. *Onward!*

Hugo made a conscious point of standing marine-erect and walking marine-springless as he waded into the crowd. He made his way toward Russell, who was already surrounded by several people, as were Lane and Buchwald, in separate circles.

Russell's eyes went immediately to Hugo's Silver Star pin. "Well, I gotta tell ya, you are certainly out of place with me," he said to Hugo, shaking his hand. "I had to lie and cheat just to win the Good Conduct medal."

Lane was next. He, too, saw the Silver Star and motioned for the others to make room for Hugo. He said, "You win that in Vietnam?"

Hugo nodded but then moved on to the Buchwald circle before Lane or anybody else could ask a follow-up. That had been his strategy for this reception. Be seen, greeted, and honored, confirm Vietnam, but don't engage long enough for specific questions. Those included even "What outfit?" Although, if unavoidable, he would say only "Ninth Marines." If someone said that was his regiment, too, Hugo would quickly ask, "What battalion?" If the questioner said, "One-Nine," then Hugo would say he was in Three-Nine. Otherwise, he would say One-Nine.

Blocking his way to Buchwald was Matt the Bear Claw cop.

He said, "Is that you, the clothing guy from the Thai restaurant? I forget your name. You've lost some weight, shaved your head . . . if that *is* you?"

Hugo said in the best rendition of his new Marine Talk, "If you're talking about a Nash Brothers clothing salesman, that's me. I just decided to get myself back into marine shape. What was *your* name again?"

"Hey, hey, good for you," said Matt. "I'm

Matt Columbia."

Hugo wanted to shout, "Semper Fi!" as loud as he could.

"I'm off on a big assignment tonight for several weeks," said Matt. "But maybe when I get back we could get together — swap marine stories and whatever."

"Sounds great. Where you headed?"

"It's an illegal wildlife case in South America," said Matt. "A lot of Americans — including some fancy ones — buy, sell, and collect exotic bird feathers and various body parts. It's all very hush-hush for now."

Hugo said he wouldn't breathe a word. And they parted.

"Hey, look here," said Art Buchwald when Hugo finally made it into his circle. "A *real* hero."

Then to Hugo, he said, "God, I wish I looked like a former marine the way you do, fella."

The first thing Hugo did when he got home was Google "shit on a shingle."

Much to his surprise and delight, up came several listings.

There was a definition from something called the Wiktionary, which described itself as "the free dictionary":

**Shit on a shingle** (sometimes abbreviated S.O.S.) is a U.S. Armed Forces slang term for chipped beef on toast. Due to the (largely) unfavorable reaction to the "cuisine" provided them, the U.S. soldiers during World War I coined this term of "affection."

There was even a recipe at www.foodrules.com:

## SHIT ON A SHINGLE

4 ½ oz. dried beef
2 cups milk
2 tbs. butter
¼ cup flour
Salt and pepper
6 slices of bread

Melt butter in pan; add dried beef. Cook 2–3 minutes until brown. Add milk (reserve 1/4 cup for later), salt, and pepper. Bring to boil. Mix flour and remaining milk together. Slowly add boiling mixture until it begins to thicken. Serve over toast.

After having so easily and quickly acquired this information, Hugo realized how important the Web had become to his life as a former marine.

He turned all aglow with thoughts about the possibility of even more great experiences tomorrow, when he reported for jury duty.

*Move out!*

# Six

Hugo had gone through the doors and the metal detectors of the H. Carl Moultrie Courthouse several times to perform jury service. But this was his first entrance as a former marine with a Silver Star pin in his coat lapel.

"Hey, man, welcome to our courthouse," said a uniformed D.C. government security guard, a tall, husky black man in his late forties. "Silver Stars are always welcome here."

Hugo extended his hand and the man shook it.

On the escalator ride up to the second-floor check-in and waiting rooms, a short elderly white man just ahead of him turned and said, "Thank you."

"For what, sir?" Hugo said. But he knew exactly what the man was talking about.

"For doing whatever you did to win that Silver Star," said the man. "I'm Judge Mc-

Illhenny — I was in the navy. Cold War between Korea and Vietnam. You?"

"Marines, sir. Vietnam."

"We swabbies always called you gyrenes our private police force," said the judge, smiling.

Hugo smiled back. He figured that must be some inside joke between the sailors and the marines. Neither swabbies nor gyrenes had been in any of his materials.

Be careful. It served as a good reminder that, last night's Smithsonian success aside, there was still an awful lot he didn't know about being a former marine.

But he did know how to be a District of Columbia juror.

D.C. had a one-day or one-trial rule. You showed up on a certain day at a certain time, and if you weren't chosen for a jury by the end of the day, you were free to go until you were summoned again in two and a half to three years. If you were selected, then you stayed until the trial ended, whether it be a day or two or a month or two.

The system worked and stood out as one of the few things about the government of the District of Columbia that did. Long lines, lost correspondence, idiotic procedures, and rude employees had long been the hallmark — and the unpleasant joke — of doing business with what passed for city hall. Hugo once spent four and a half hours waiting in line just to get his driver's license renewed. But there had always been one dramatic exception to the rule: the D.C. Superior Court, where both civil and criminal law cases were tried and resolved.

Hugo went first to a short line — short because prospective jurors were given staggered times to report. He moved through an office to show his jury summons, check in, and get a plastic-covered cardboard badge to wear. It had JUROR in large blue block letters. A number above that would be his identity as long as he was on jury duty.

He walked toward the huge juror waiting room at the end of the hall.

"Hugo . . . Hugo Marder, is that you?"

The voice was familiar. Female. Michigan. Wife. *Ex*-wife. Emily.

He turned. "Yes, Emily, this is me."

She also had a JUROR badge attached to her jacket, the top of a two-piece dark brown gabardine suit that Hugo recognized. Emily had never been into clothes and never understood why Hugo was. "It's my job!" he'd said to her more than once.

"What have you done to your hair — your

head, for God's sake?" she said.

Nothing had happened to her hair or to her appearance since the last time he'd seen her, which was nearly three years ago. That encounter was at the Kennedy Center and, like this one, an accident. She was still five feet five inches tall and too thin; her hair was still red and short; her wide face was still freckled, her eyes blue, her smile tight.

"I removed it," Hugo said of his hair.

A peculiar look came over her face. It was the one she got when she was confused, which wasn't that often — at least while she was married to Hugo.

"What have you done with your*self?* You've lost . . . well, weight."

"Thanks for noticing," Hugo said.

"You're talking like somebody else, too. Somebody who . . . well . . ."

"Matters?"

"Yeah, that's it."

"You bailed out too soon, Emily. You could have had this new, improved model."

"We can sit together." She took a step.

"Nope," he said, moving with her.

"Why not?"

"You *had* your chance to sit with me."

"Jesus, Hugo," she said, her voice rising slightly. There were people passing by them in the hall, but it was noisy and nobody was paying any attention to them, much less listening to what they were saying. "I've never seen you like this. You even walk differently."

"I've never been like this, Emily."

He was about to add something edgy about how the return to single life had given him a jolt to spring forward in new ways when he suddenly remembered the Silver Star pin in his coat lapel. *Damn!*

Ways to get it out of there were racing through his mind when Emily said, "What is that pin you're wearing?"

She stopped and touched his left arm to stop him. Then she stepped out in front and faced him. Grabbing his lapel, she said, "Is that some kind of medal?"

"Boy Scout," he said, his forceful marine presence withering.

"No, it isn't. I've seen it before. It's for heroism. A military thing. The Bronze Star, Silver Star — something like that. Right, right. Congressman Richards, a right-winger from Texas, wears one. He got it in Korea. Right, right. The Silver Star."

She brought her face closer toward his. "What are you up to, Hugo?" she said in a near-whisper.

Hugo thought of the Marine Hymn. The words of Art Buchwald. *I wish I looked like a former marine the way you do, fella.*

Hugo considered telling her the truth. And then he would reach down, thrust his hands around her neck, and strangle her. He definitely had the marine strength of body and mind to do it. If somebody noticed and cared, so be it. They could have the arrest, arraignment, trial, and sentencing right here on the courthouse premises. One-stop criminal justice in action.

"It's none of your business, Emily. You're out of my life. Stay out of it." His volume was louder than hers. But still, nobody else cared or heard.

"You can't go around wearing a Silver Star you didn't really win. I'll bet it's against the law, for one thing. It's immoral, for another. It's outrageous. It's so un-you. Are you on drugs? Drinking?"

*Marines move out.* That's what Matt had said.

"Fuck you, Emily," Hugo said, and strode on into the waiting room.

Marrying Emily had been the biggest mistake of his life. Not only had she walked out on him, she'd taken with her several little pieces of his esteem and self-respect, maybe even some of his soul.

Was he trying to replace what she'd swiped

with a transplant of sorts? Maybe instead of implanting an exact replica, such as a heart for a heart or a kidney for a kidney, he was doing it with something entirely different — and much larger. A whole nonentity clothing salesman would be replaced by a whole former marine.

Hugo and Emily had met at a Michigan Western mixer, but nothing had happened. There had been no spark and no dating and definitely no igniting. It was only after they went to the same working-singles party on a below-zero blizzardy night in Big Rapids that the relationship really began. He had begun to carry a small sketchbook with him, and she had been most impressed when he drew her face in a few seconds with a charcoal pencil.

Later, Hugo concluded — often and seriously — that the sketch and a mutual winter's-night need for body heat from another human being had driven them together. There wasn't even much obvious compatibility or shared aspiration in their respective life stories.

Hugo told Emily that even though he'd been a business major, he had really wanted to be an artist, not one who painted with oils or watercolor but a cartoonist who created with a pencil or pen. His heroes were

Charles Schulz, Mort Walker, and Hank Ketcham. He'd taken every art and drawing course he could and had done some drawing for his high school and the Michigan Western student newspapers. One of his works, a four-panel comic strip making fun of students who waited until the last minute to study for exams, had won third place in a regional collegiate journalism competition. But after graduation, he couldn't find a job with a newspaper or magazine in Michigan — the only place he looked — so he joined the graphics department of a small religious publisher in Big Rapids, mostly doing sketches for book covers and advertising brochures. It was enjoyable work.

She asked him what had happened with the cartooning. He told her the truth. His drawings were fine, but his narratives and funny lines weren't so hot.

"Why not do some hard-hitting political cartoons that really go after the Democrats as tax-and-spend liberals who care more about unions than the country?" Emily asked. "I've seen some that say more in one picture than thousands of words in an editorial."

"Politics isn't really my thing, but I'll think about it," Hugo replied.

Politics was more than a mere thing to

Emily. It was an obsession. She told Hugo she had worked as a volunteer for candidates since she was in junior high, had majored in political science at Michigan Western, and now had a full-time job in the district office of a Republican congressman. Hugo thought even on that first night that it was too bad Johnny Aldrich had died in the parachute accident, because he and Emily were made for each other. Hugo and Emily were not. But they got married anyhow, in a small Methodist ceremony in Emily's hometown of Muskegon, Michigan.

Hugo did try some political cartoons, but Emily dismissed them as "too soft" or "too naïve." He agreed with her. She offered to collaborate. She would supply the punchy ideas and lines, and he would do the drawings. But that didn't interest Hugo, and the idea never got off the ground.

Then one afternoon Emily shouted over the phone to Hugo, "I've been offered a job in the Washington office!"

Hugo, contented in Big Rapids, did not want to move to Washington. He still harbored the belief that one day he would break out as a cartoonist, but always here in Big Rapids. He could do his drawing right here and send his cartoons off to New York or wherever. He was a Michigan boy who had no need to get out of this town, to go away to find his life, his future, his worth. But Emily wore him down with much talk about the new world, where it was the woman's turn to have her husband put aside his aspirations in favor of his wife's. He finally said, "Fine. Okay. Let's go to Washington."

They moved to a rented basement apartment on Capitol Hill — tiny, compared to what they'd had in Michigan for much less money — and Hugo went out looking for a job as a graphic artist. Cartooning, even on the side, was over. It made him feel particularly irresponsible to even consider drawing pictures at home while his wife was out working and he was not.

"Do something else, then," said Emily after four weeks of Hugo's unsuccessful job hunting.

"Such as?"

"What does it matter? You've got to work, Hugo."

*What does it matter?*

It was a put-down that caused a rip in him that never scabbed over.

One morning two weeks later, while scanning the *Washington Post* classifieds, he saw the advertisement that eventually led him to

Nash Brothers.

ARE YOU A QUALITY MAN?
ARE YOU INTERESTED IN A QUALITY
CAREER SELLING CLOTHES TO OTHER
QUALITY MEN?

That was the headline. Hugo didn't necessarily see himself as a quality man, but there had always been something about clothes that interested him. Back in high school, he was described in the Newton High annual as being "tall, skinny, quiet, and a sharp dresser." Even then he had an appreciation for creases in pants, buttons in holes, shoes with shines. He didn't know where it came from, it was just in him. But it also carried over into his drawing. All of his cartoon characters were always well dressed.

There was an immediate sensation of belonging the first time he walked into the Nash Brothers store at Nineteenth and L. It had a comfortable feel, an aroma of fine cloth and good leather, a look of honest and caring people, an atmosphere of high and proud standards.

As a sales associate trainee, he learned the differences in feel, longevity, and care needs between a 100 percent wool suit, say, and one that was 80 percent wool and 20 percent polyester. He was taught that some men were born to wear double-breasted suits, while some should never do so. There were similar ideal choices to be made between two-button and three-button suit coats and about whether a vest was appropriate. Sizes were important, particularly in deciding whether the gentleman required a short, regular, or long. The same applied to various lapel, shoulder, and cuff styles and even to whether a pair of trousers should have a pleated or plain front. Pleats on short men might make them look overweight. On tall men, they worked the other way.

Hugo became a man who knew and appreciated the meaning of worsted, twill, twist, blend, two-ply, travel-weight, wrinkle-resistant, herringbone, and countless other words of the trade.

His idea had been to sell clothes only for a while, until something in graphics turned up. He didn't tell anybody at Nash Brothers that, of course. As far as they knew, he was coming aboard for life, and that was pretty much what had happened.

Hugo, over time, accepted and then lived the most common of American male rationalizations. Yes, the first things we're taught in school are drawing, writing stories, singing, dancing, performing, reciting, and playing sports. All of them are skills that, if extraordinary and honed, can lead to gold — fame and fortune. And creative satisfaction. No kid, when asked, says he wants to grow up and sell men's clothes. But slowly, for most, all of the big dreams get set aside. *Be practical.* Think of ordinary life and ordinary things such as Michigan Bell, banks, business, teaching, marriage, children, houses, church, Rotary, settling down. Life is not a dream.

Hugo had known a guy at Michigan Western who played the trumpet like Harry James. He was so good and so obviously destined for stardom that everybody called him Harry, even though his real name was Thomas. But after college and two years in the army, Thomas came back to his hometown, a small place near Battle Creek, and took over his dying father's hardware store. A short while later, Hugo read in the *Big Rapids Post* that Thomas had shot and killed his mother, two of his seven employees, and himself. The story didn't say anything about the trumpet or Harry James, but Hugo read it there anyhow.

Hugo wasn't the killer type — then. But if he had been, he would have exterminated Emily's congressional-staffer friends. Their parties, always loud and spontaneous and so, so special — to them — were awful. Their eyes and minds glassed over at meeting Hugo. These were people who wanted only to be with people involved in politics, issues, governments, things that *mattered.* They were pretty people on the move, ambitious young people who worshipped famous old people, little people who believed it was only a matter of time until they were big.

It was after one of these parties that Emily ended the marriage.

Hugo had gone to the party with new and good intentions. Instead of standing off from the little group discussions and laughs about the major people and issues of the day, he decided to try playing the game.

"Dalton Andrews is a regular customer of mine," Hugo, after declaring that he sold clothes for Nash Brothers, ventured to a young man who was an assistant to a legislative assistant to a Missouri congressman.

"I'll keep you in mind," said the young man. "Someday I'll be buying all my clothes at Nash Brothers."

And the kid ran away. He had better things to talk about, better people to talk to.

Back at home later, Hugo repeated the story to Emily and expressed the severe annoyance it had aroused in him.

She replied, "You should have told him you were with the CIA, the FCC, or something. Or even a cartoonist. Nobody has the time or interest to talk to a clothing salesman. That's just the truth."

"Is it the truth for you, too?"

"Yes, I guess it is. I thought I was marrying an artistic type. Somebody who could draw. I think it makes sense for us to call it quits. We're about as compatible as Ford and Reagan."

And that was it. Emily kept the apartment on the Hill, and Hugo moved out; first to a small place and eventually to his town house with the red door on Nineteenth Street. The split was amicable and quick. There would be no alimony, no lingering ties or aches.

Hugo gave only a passing thought to returning to Big Rapids. He also toyed, briefly and halfheartedly, with the idea of taking up drawing again. But it really was too late, for both Big Rapids and drawing. Besides, he was comfortable with and quite proud of being Hugo Marder, sales associate at the Nash Brothers store in Washington, D.C., the capital of the United States of America.

The only good things Emily let him take were their desktop computer and the basic skills of using and appreciating it that she had painstakingly taught him. After she left, he late-blossomed into his present state as a semi-nerd who constantly browsed the fun and many wonders of the Internet.

He had yet to experience one conscious moment of missing Emily or anything about her.

Whenever he came to the jury room, Hugo was reminded of the old Greyhound–Indian Trails bus depot in Kalamazoo. The noise, the clutter, the odors, the people rushing around were almost the same.

So was the seating. There were some twenty-five rows of stationary seats on either side of an aisle three yards wide. Most were occupied this morning, as usual, with people reading books or the *Post* or eating and drinking vending-machine fare while watching the television mounted on the wall at the far end and tuned to CNN.

Hugo took a vacant seat between two men, an elderly black and a younger Latino. He sensed Emily had been right behind him, but she didn't even give him a glance as she marched farther down the aisle to a seat. Hugo was certain — he just could tell — that it was taking every bit of restraint she had to refrain from shooting him the finger. When they were married, she did that a lot — in fun, of course. *Of course.*

But, once seated, Hugo realized with alarm that Emily now presented a serious danger. She could, at any time, blow the whistle on his posing, his fraud. She might really turn him in to the FBI if, as she said, it was illegal to wear another man's medal. Whatever, her ability to cause problems and make mischief would be a source of anxiety every day he was in Washington.

But *only* in Washington. He knew in a flash what he needed to do. Move to another city! He must give his new start a new environment, free of people like Emily who might place him in jeopardy.

He wouldn't have to leave Nash Brothers. The company had stores in eleven major U.S. cities. What about New York? Too big. San Francisco? Too expensive. Los Angeles? Too spread out. Chicago? Too cold. Dallas? *Dallas.* Hugo had never been there, but it seemed to have the right feel, and he knew the Nash Brothers store was in a well-established shopping center called North-Park.

Hugo would speak to Jackson Dyer tomorrow about transferring to Dallas, assuming he was not selected for a jury.

*Move out!*

He reached into his coat pocket for his

paperback copy of *Marine Rifleman: Forty-three Years in the Corps,* the memoir of retired marine general Wesley Fox. A quote on the back from *The Journal of Military History* said, "Fox was, and still is, the Marine all of us wanted to be. . . . This book explains why." Hugo could only say amen to that. Fox had enlisted during the Korean War when he was eighteen and, among other things, won the Medal of Honor ten years later in Vietnam while leading a rifle company in One-Nine. That, of course, was Ron Cunningham's outfit and, as of now, Hugo's.

Hugo had flipped through the book quickly and was reading it a second time with more care. But before opening it now, he looked around at his fellow jurors. Jury duty was the great equalizer in Washington, because the famous and powerful couldn't afford the bad publicity that would go with trying to pull strings to be excused. That was Hugo's theory, at least. One time he'd seen David Brinkley in this room; Brinkley could have gotten anybody to do anything he wanted. Another time Hugo got a glimpse of a woman who did the weather on Channel 4.

Isn't that Ben Bradlee over there? Hugo thought the man with the slicked-back hair across the aisle and six rows down who was engrossed in doing a newspaper crossword puzzle sure did look like the great former *Washington Post* editor of Watergate fame. Jason Robards, Jr., had played him in a movie. Or was it Robert Redford?

Hugo wasn't about to go over and strike up a conversation with Mr. Bradlee. He wouldn't do that under any circumstances, anywhere, but particularly not here. There was an unspoken rule that nobody bothered anyone else in this jury room. Everyone passed the time the way he or she wished — reading, writing notes, napping, daydreaming. Whatever. Nobody came to jury service with the expectation of having a chat. Silence was the rule, except when asked an official question by someone involved in the official process.

As Hugo opened his book, a video explaining jury service came up on the television. Hugo had seen it before, so he continued reading a section in which Fox, then a first lieutenant, reported for assignment at the Third Marine Division headquarters in Vietnam. A personnel captain gave Fox the option of going to One-Nine.

" 'Have you not heard of the Walking Dead?'

" 'No,' I answered, expecting a sea story.

" 'One-Nine is known as the Walking Dead. They had heavy contacts and had taken many casualties. Several companies were all but annihilated on Khe Sanh. Did you never hear of that? A corporal was the commander for a while. No one wants to go to that battalion. If you do — regardless of rank — stick around long enough, meaning stay alive, and you'll end up as the commander.' "

Hugo kept reading for another twenty minutes or so, until a young black woman came to the podium at the front of the room. Over a microphone, she began calling out juror numbers. These would be the members of the next panel to be sent to a courtroom, she said. They were to line up outside in a single line and then follow a court officer to the courtroom, where they would be questioned, screened, chosen, or rejected. Hugo knew the drill.

"Five-six-three, six-nine-three," said the jury official eventually. That was Hugo's number.

He closed his book, stood and moved toward the hallway. So, unfortunately, did Emily.

He said a silent prayer: Please, Dear God of Juries, do not put me on a jury with this woman.

The courtroom was small and felt even smaller because of its low ceilings. Every piece of wood in the room, including the judge's bench and all the furniture, was shellacked to a shiny natural blond. Hugo had read a story in the *Post* once that said the decorating style of most D.C. court-rooms was "fifties Holiday Inn." That sounded right to Hugo, who had been in several.

Emily, thank God, was sitting six or seven down in the churchlike pew, one of several used by spectators during trials. Every space was taken now with prospective jurors, as was the twelve-seat jury box, down front inside the rail on the right. The attorneys, both prosecution and defense, were at tables, with the judge's higher bench in the middle. All standard courtroom arrange-ment.

"All rise!" yelled a bailiff. "Superior Court for the District of Columbia is now in ses-sion, Judge T. W. McIllhenny presiding."

It was the judge from the escalator. The navy man. Now wearing a black robe, he entered the room from a door on the left and behind the bench.

Hugo was suddenly keyed up. Here was a judge of the Superior Court who would soon realize that he had in his jury panel a former marine who had won the Silver Star in Vietnam. And that person was . . . well, *Hugo!*

Judge McIllhenny, once seated, smiled and then slowly and silently surveyed the assembled citizens of the District of Columbia. When the judge's gaze came to Hugo, who was sitting barely fifteen yards away, his eyes brightened. He nodded to Hugo.

"On behalf of the Superior Court of the District of Columbia, I welcome you and I thank you," said the judge to everyone. "You are performing a citizen's single most important service to his or her community. To come here, in a court of law, and judge the guilt or innocence of another citizen is the highest of civic callings. I commend you for answering the call."

Hugo recognized the message as essentially the same delivered to all jury panels. It was followed by an explanation of the process.

The judge told them, "First several yes-or-no questions will be asked. Each will be answered by raising your right hand. Then, after consultations with attorneys, some of you may be excused to return to the jury lounge for possible service to another court. Do not go home! The day is still young. The remaining jurors will then be questioned one at a time, in private. Eventually, twelve of you will be chosen to serve on the jury, with two more as alternates."

Voir dire was next. The judge told them that the alleged crime was an assault with a deadly weapon. A male defendant stood accused of firing a .38-caliber pistol at another man, hitting him in the stomach. Hugo and his fifty-plus fellow prospective jurors looked at the defense table as a tall, muscular white man in a dark suit, white shirt, and tie raised his right hand.

"Do any of you know this man?" asked the judge. After stating the defendant's name and the location, date, and time of the alleged crime, McIllhenny asked if anyone on the jury panel had witnessed or in any way participated in the event.

No hands went up.

Then came a series of questions aimed at finding out if members of the juror pool knew any of the defendant's family, investigating police officers, witnesses, lawyers, or anyone else involved in the case. These questions were followed by more general ones on attitudes about the police, firearms, and the like.

Hugo didn't count them, but he thought there had been at least twenty-five questions by the time the judge asked the last one. Hugo had raised his hand only once, and that was on the general lawyer question. He knew that several of his See Yous practiced some kind of law, even if, like Secretary Dalton Andrews, it was mostly of a political nature.

After consulting with the lawyers, Judge McIllhenny read out fourteen juror numbers. "Return to the lounge, please," he said.

After a prayer to the God of Jurors, Hugo looked to his right, hoping to see Emily rising from her seat to leave.

No. She not only wasn't on the move, she caught his glance and smiled at him.

Then the judge, the defendant, and the lawyers retired to the jury room directly behind the court, where individual voir dire would be conducted.

Hugo returned to *Marine Rifleman* and stayed with it except for an occasional look around the courtroom to see what was going on. Nothing much ever was. Most everyone was doing what he was doing. Even Emily, who seldom read anything outside of newspapers and position papers, seemed engrossed in a paperback book. He couldn't make out the title. He assumed it was about politics. That was all that interested this woman.

Fox's memoir completely absorbed him. The general matter-of-factly recounted the events that led to his being awarded the Medal of Honor, and then said, "I do not feel that my actions were deserving of such recognition."

Outside thoughts drifted by occasionally. For a few seconds, Hugo tried to imagine the taste of shit on a shingle. He couldn't. He thought about giving the recipe a try sometime. Maybe when he moved to Dallas.

Then a bailiff shouted out his juror number.

Then, like a hot wind through a narrow door, came the realization that things were about to get serious. Now he would be speaking directly to a judge who thought he was a real marine hero.

Soon he was sitting at a table in a closed room, prepared to answer questions, under oath in private, from Judge McIllhenny and the lawyers on both sides.

The defendant, who sat at the far end of the table, looked to be in his late forties or early fifties, mean, and very much like a man who could take a shot at somebody. An armed officer sat next to and slightly behind the defendant. A woman straddling a steno machine sat to the side.

"I'd love to hear the story behind that Silver Star, Mr. Marder," said the judge, "but I guess that'll have to wait for another occasion."

Thank you, God of Jurors, thought Hugo. At least he would be spared the potential trauma of having to tell his phony marine story to a judge of the Superior Court of the District of Columbia.

The judge asked Hugo about his raised hand on knowing lawyers. Hugo quickly explained that he was a Nash Brothers sales associate, and as such, had many customers who practiced law.

"Does that make you love lawyers or hate lawyers?" asked one of the two defense attorneys, an older black man.

Everyone, including the judge, laughed.

"If they buy clothes, I love them, and if they don't, I hate them," Hugo answered. Then he contemplated his spontaneous, witty, knowing response.

The old Hugo Marder never would have done that — never *could* have done that.

*Semper Fi and Move out!*

The judge told Hugo he could return to his seat in the courtroom. Then he stood to shake Hugo's hand, an action that clearly surprised the lawyers but was a delight for Hugo.

The lawyers, seeming to feel it was the correct and expected thing for them to do also, jumped to their feet.

"Everybody put their hands above their heads! That includes you, Judge. You, cop. And you, hero."

It was the defendant. He was holding a very large pistol. Where in the hell did he get that? Hugo thought.

As Hugo put his hands in the air, he caught a glimpse of the policeman's empty holster. While he and everyone else had been distracted by the fuss over the guy with the Silver Star, this thug had grabbed the gun.

"Back there in the corner — all of you except the judge and the hero."

The gunman moved up along the far side of the table, toward Hugo and Judge Mc-Illhenny.

"Where did you win that Silver Star?" he barked at Hugo. His voice was deep, menacing.

"Vietnam."

"What service? I was there."

"Marines."

The gunman started to smile and to say

something. Was he going to say "Semper Fi"? Oh my God. Hugo reminded himself that not all former marines were in the same league as Russell, Buchwald, and Lane. There were also the Oswald and Whitman types.

But this guy, as if coming to grips with the obvious fact that this was neither a smiling nor a Semper Fi occasion, just said, "What outfit?"

"The Ninth Marines."

"I was in One-Nine. They wiped us out at Khe Sanh. Only three of us in my platoon came out of that fucking hell alive."

Hugo, his newly hatched contingency lines clicking in, said, "I was in *Two*-Nine. It was bad, but not as bad as it was for you guys — the Walking Dead."

"The Walking Dead. Yeah. That's what they named us."

The gunman still stood to the side of the table, so he could keep an eye on the others, but he had gradually inched up to within a few feet of Hugo and the judge.

"That's what you are right now, Judge," the gunman said, suddenly pointing the pistol at McIllhenny's head. "The walking dead — that's you."

Hugo, his heart pumping, took the deepest breath of his life and said, "Hand me the gun and let's end this. You'll never get out of here alive."

"I wish I hadn't gotten out of Vietnam. The judge ain't walking out of here, that's all that matters. You remember Richie Anderson, Judge? A kid of eighteen. You sent him to prison for life five years ago. He wasn't guilty of anything. He was set up by a bunch of drug gang punks. They told you, but you wouldn't listen. I was sitting in that fucking courtroom and heard it all. Richie's already been turned into some monster's pussycat in prison. I can't kill the monster, so I'm going to kill you."

"No, no," said Hugo.

"Yes, yes," said the gunman. "My serial number was four-five-seven-eight-nine-oh. Yours?"

"Oh-eight-one-two-seven-eight."

"A fucking officer?"

Hugo thought he would now be shot for being a fucking officer. He remembered what Mark Russell had said in jest about hating officers. *In jest?*

But the gunman kept the weapon on the judge. "I couldn't believe my luck in drawing you as my judge, and then a minute ago that dumb cop not paying attention . . ."

Hugo heard a click. It came from the gun. Had the man cocked it?

Without a further thought, Hugo sprang his newly trimmed and exercised body off the floor and forward, his arms and hands stretched out before him.

He felt the metal of the pistol against his own right hand. There was a loud, jarring bang. He felt something resembling the force of a speeding truck crash into his right shoulder as he fell on top of his fellow former marine.

That was all he felt until he regained consciousness in a VIP room at the Washington City Medical Center.

# SEVEN

Emily. He heard her voice before he saw her.

"He moved his eyelids," she said to someone.

"It shouldn't be long now," said another woman.

Hugo blinked. He felt some discomfort in his right shoulder. "I'm moving to Dallas," he mumbled.

"He's hallucinating," Emily said to somebody. "Nobody moves to Dallas."

"I'm going to go get the doctor." It was the same woman he had heard before.

Hugo felt a pair of lips down against his right ear. They had a familiar feel. They were Emily's.

"Don't worry, Hugo," she whispered. "Your secret is safe with me. You're a real hero this time. I'm so proud."

*Real* hero?

Keeping his eyes closed, he began remembering. The courtroom. The jury room. Judge McIllhenny. The voir dire. The former marine with the gun. One-Nine. The Walking Dead. The leap. The noise. The whop in the shoulder.

"*The Washington Herald* did a big story. 'Once a hero, always a hero,' that kind of thing. I talked to the reporter — a woman named Winfield. She was in the courthouse when it happened. I told her you won the Silver Star as a marine in Vietnam. She wanted details, but I told her you never wanted to talk about it."

"So how's our hero doing?" It was a man's voice.

Hugo figured it was time to come out of it. He opened his eyes to see a bushy-haired man of forty or so in a white coat leaning over him.

"Welcome back, Mr. Marder," he said. "I'm Reg Moore — I had the pleasure of doing the heavy lifting on you. You were out of this world for almost twenty hours."

"Thank you, Doctor," Hugo said. "What did you have to do?"

"Pretty major surgery on that shoulder. I had to keep you under anesthesia for a while, and that meant you slept longer after we were finished."

Hugo could smell Emily. She had moved

around to the other side of the bed. A nurse was standing with her.

"You are really something, Hugo," Emily said.

Hugo smelled flowers. Who would have sent him flowers? The store. Yes, the men at the store. Jackson Dyer probably had collected some money from everyone.

The doctor pulled a bandage away from Hugo's right shoulder. "It's coming right along," he said. "No infection, no complications. The bullet went right through, took some stuff with it, but you'll be as good as new and up and about in no time."

"Good," Hugo said.

"Great!" Emily said.

"Can I do anything for you?" asked Dr. Moore.

Hugo shook his head.

"Well, the hospital has scheduled a news briefing about you in ten minutes. I need to get down there." The doctor patted Hugo lightly on the arm and left the room.

A few seconds later, the nurse excused herself. "I'll let you and Mrs. Marder have some private time," she said.

*Mrs. Marder?*

"Mrs. Marder?" Hugo echoed to Emily after the nurse had cleared the door.

Emily came close. "I had to let them think

we were still married."

"You didn't call yourself Mrs. Marder even when we were married."

"I know, I know. But they wouldn't let me in the room if I wasn't family."

Hugo tried to fight off a laugh — a guffaw, really.

"This is really exciting, Hugo. I couldn't miss it. Now we're both living lies . . . so to speak. I don't tell yours, and you don't tell mine. Deal?"

Hugo had only to fight off a slight smile this time. He said, "What's the news briefing the doctor was talking about?"

"You are big, big news. The local TV channels and news radio stations are all over the story. Frederick Lane even wants to do a major piece on his network news program. One of his producers asked me to ask if you would do an interview with him. He said Lane knew you. You know Frederick Lane? Is he a customer of yours?"

Hugo felt warmth throughout his wounded body. It was bad enough to have a story in the *Herald.* But a *national* television story? No way.

"Tell them no, I don't want to talk about it. And tell them I would respectfully request that they do no story at all, even one without my interview."

Emily said she would pass on the message. "I get why you don't want a lot of publicity."

Hugo, for the first time, looked carefully around the room, which was larger than any he had ever seen in a hospital. There were several arrangements of flowers.

"The flowers," he said. "Who sent them?"

"You won't believe it, but those over there — the red roses — came from Art Buchwald. *The* Art Buchwald. The note with it said, 'You really are a hero.' There's another from Mark Russell, you know, the funny guy. All he said was: 'Eat a lot of S.O.S. and you'll be fine.' Why would those two send you flowers? Are they customers? What's S.O.S.?"

Hugo decided not to tell her a damn thing. She could call herself Mrs. Marder if she wanted to, but he didn't have to treat her as if she really were. "Who else sent flowers?"

"Judge McIllhenny. Nash Brothers here. Nash Brothers headquarters in New York. Robert, for himself and his family. Some guy who runs a Thai restaurant — I thought you hated Thai food? A Melinda somebody. Who's she?"

"I met her in Sunday school," Hugo said. "She's a CIA agent."

"I don't believe you. When did you start going to Sunday school?"

Hugo only smiled.

"Oh my God," Emily squealed. She was excited. "I almost forgot." She ran over to a credenza and returned with a silver-framed eight-by-ten photograph. It was Dalton Andrews. "Look what he wrote there in the corner — in his own handwriting."

Emily shoved the picture close enough for Hugo to see. It was a seated portrait of Secretary Andrews with the U.S. flag over his right shoulder and the flag of the secretary of defense over his left.

Hugo read the inscription:

"To my friend Hugo — with admiration for your deeds and your modesty, Dalton Andrews."

Then, below that as a kind of P.S., "Recognize the coat?"

It was a dark blue, almost black, cashmere blazer with a gold-and-black-striped silk lining that Hugo had sold Mr. Andrews nearly twelve years ago, when he was still a 46R.

"I knew he was a customer," said Emily. "But it never occurred to me that he actually knew your name."

Hugo closed his eyes and made no response.

"I really am so, so proud of you, Hugo.

Isn't it wonderful for us?"

He had worked hard to train himself for being a phony hero. He had not prepared to be a real one, particularly in tandem with and in the company of Emily.

Hugo was presented the District of Columbia Medal of Honor in a ceremony held at the canteen on his hospital floor.

Emily and some forty hospital and Superior Court personnel were there. Hugo, dressed in fresh dark blue Nash Brothers pajamas and a white terry-cloth robe, sat in a wheelchair on one side of the rectangular room, directly in front of the vending machines, refrigerator, and microwave.

Judge McIllhenny stood on Hugo's right, the Washington mayor Barry Hechinger on the left. "As chance would have it, I ran into Mr. Marder on the escalator that morning before court," said Judge McIllhenny. "I noted the Silver Star in his lapel, thanked him for his service to country, and, after some more talk about marines and sailors, I said, 'Our nation needs more heroes.' "

The crowd interrupted with applause. Somebody yelled out, "Amen!" Another person yelled, "You can say that again!"

"Little did I know," continued the judge, "that Mr. Marder, barely two hours later, was going to honor my wish by demonstrating that personal heroism is no accident. It is a character trait — and, for Mr. Marder, clearly a permanent reflex."

More applause.

"I was in that jury room, ladies and gentlemen. I not only witnessed his heroism, I was the beneficiary of it. Had he not acted, I most likely would not be standing here — or anywhere else — today.

"Thank you, Mr. Marder," he said, looking down at Hugo. "There are many forms and manifestations of debts, sir. I owe you the ultimate debt. I owe you my life."

Judge McIllhenny, his eyes now full of tears, nodded across Hugo to the mayor, a tall, thin, light-skinned black man of fifty whose major trademarks were bow ties and short speeches. He was also an energetic advocate of statehood for the District of Columbia, which he emphasized, among other means, by saying to almost everyone when greeting them, "Call me Governor-elect."

"I am here as the representative of your fellow and sister citizens of the District of Columbia, otherwise known as the vote-deprived fellow and sister members of America's last colony," said the mayor to Hugo.

There was applause, but only a smattering. Most of these people, thought Hugo, probably lived in the Maryland or northern Virginia suburbs and probably thought a state of D.C. was a lousy idea.

The mayor said, still addressing Hugo, "There is nothing more precious than human life, and thus, there can be nothing more noble than the saving of human life."

It was only then that Hugo saw what the mayor had in his hands: a small case that resembled the one for Ron Cunningham's — *his* — Silver Star.

Mayor Hechinger opened it and showed Hugo what was inside. It was the same arrangement as in the Silver Star case: a ribbon mounted at the top, then the medal hanging on a larger piece of ribbon, and a lapel pin below that. The ribbons and the pin were red and white — the official colors of the District — and the medal was round, about the size of a silver dollar, and bronze.

"There is more than one kind of medal of honor, sir. While not in the league with the main Medal of Honor, I would submit that the District of Columbia Medal of Honor is definitely in the same ballpark. Both are the highest honors the government can award, and both honor individuals for bravery and courage under fire."

The mayor turned away from Hugo. "I would ask now that Mrs. Marder please step forward to pin this Medal of Honor on her husband's chest."

She is not Mrs. Marder. She is not my wife. She is my ex-wife . . .

Those words didn't even come anywhere near his mouth before passing right out of Hugo's mind. The Deal. He had made a deal of silence with Emily.

She was coiffed and dressed better than Hugo had seen her since their wedding. Not only was she wearing a trim light blue linen suit that looked brand-new, she clearly had made a rare trip to a beauty salon. A dispassionate observer might even have thought of her as attractive — only at the thinnest of skin-deep levels, of course, and only for these few briefest of passing moments.

Hugo, preferences aside, could not help but breathe in her perfume and gaze down at her cleavage when she leaned over and pinned on the medal.

He also could not frown as she kissed him a little more than lightly on the lips while everyone in the canteen applauded.

Then the mayor handed Hugo the microphone.

This was what he had dreaded most. He had not spoken in public since high school speech class. And except to holler marching or running cadences, public speaking hadn't been on his list of things to do to become a former marine.

After many hours of sleepless anguish, he had come up with two things to say, both borrowed.

First he told an abbreviated version of Robert's story about the two young men from the Cyprus village. Hugo said, "The only thing special about me and what I did was the opportunity."

His second point was from Matt Columbia. "A former-marine acquaintance had occasion to remind me recently that marines, when confronted with a difficult situation, don't freeze. They move out. That's all I did. I moved out.

"Thank you, Mr. Mayor, for this medal. Thank you, Judge McIllhenny, for your gracious words. Thanks to all of you for coming today."

He did not thank Emily for anything.

But then, as he glanced around, he saw that she was staring at him. He did a double take. She was also moving her mouth in a most private, suggestive way, as she'd done during their married days, to signal that she was prepared, in exchange for something she wanted, to use her mouth in a fashion that would give him great pleasure.

He quickly concluded his remarks by saying, "And, of course, I wish to publicly thank Emily for being here by my side."

Late that night, after hospital lights-out, he had an occasion to thank her privately for something very specific.

After Hugo's words of appreciation, Emily said, "What was that crap you mumbled the other day about moving to Dallas?"

Her tone was old Emily. It was a demand for an answer, not a request.

"Oh, I simply decided it would be prudent to change the scene as well as my life — my life's story," said Hugo. He spoke calmly, neutrally.

"Well, *I'm* not moving to Dallas," said Emily. She said it in a way marines would call an order of the day.

The first response that came to Hugo's mind was pure Marine Talk: Who in the hell asked you?

But this was no time to say anything like that. Not yet. That could wait.

Instead, he said, "Nash Brothers has a terrific store in Dallas. It's a growing city, with good museums and transportation and climate —"

"Bullshit, Hugo! You don't give a damn

about museums. We're staying right here where we belong. I'm on the verge of becoming a congressman's chief of staff. Do you realize what an important step that is for us? Dallas? Not in your wildest dreams."

Hugo, an oh-so-happy man, allowed his eyelids to flicker and then gently fall. "Speaking of dreams," he said ever so softly, "I'm going to sleep now. Thanks again for . . . well, everything."

Dr. Reg Moore, it turned out, had been both correct and competent. The bullet that had careened through Hugo's shoulder had done some damage. But the healing of the stitch-closed holes on both sides was proceeding quickly and without complications. The doctor said Hugo should be able to return to work and the rest of his normal life within a matter of days.

"Go with the way you feel," he said when he sent Hugo home from the hospital.

Hugo's only complication was Emily. She had become a tick as well as a caring phony wife. She came to visit Hugo every evening, which he did nothing to stop. For exposure-protection reasons, he did not want to alienate Emily beyond a certain point.

She also kept him informed. She arrived

from her office each evening with the latest news on his case. The real former marine who had shot Hugo was charged with enough crimes — including attempted murder of a Superior Court judge — that, if he were convicted, would put him away for the rest of his life.

The most important news Emily brought was that the events had remained, for the most part, a local Washington story. In honor of Hugo's request, Frederick Lane never did a story. Neither did any of the other networks. Two of the cable news channels mentioned it on the day of the shooting, but, as always, their attention quickly got diverted elsewhere, and they never returned. The Associated Press moved one short account, which, according to Emily's surfing of various websites and news archives, was picked up by scores of newspapers around the country.

The major account was the *Herald* story, which ran on the front page under the headline MARINE HERO THWARTS COURTHOUSE ATTACKER. The report, written by Lisa Winfield, the reporter Emily had mentioned, was full of detail and quotes from witnesses and officials about Hugo's heroism. Hugo teared up in a major way the first time he read it. By the fourth reading, his reaction had downscaled to a slight lump rising in his throat and deep embarrassment in his soul.

On the evening before he was to leave the hospital, Emily said, "I very much like the New Hugo, a person, shaved head and potty mouth aside, I find much more attractive than the old one."

Too bad the reverse isn't true! You're still the same Old Emily! That's what Hugo thought but did not say. He said nothing.

"Maybe we should remarry," she said, as casually as proposing a new restaurant to try.

"Considering our history, do you really believe that would be in our joint and individual best interests?" he said, as gently as he could manage.

"Our history happened before you became a hero — a somebody, Hugo," she said, still in her old Emily-the-boss mode.

Hugo had mistakenly assumed that once she had soaked in the full reflective benefits from what he had done and become, she would be gone like a flash.

He went to his last line of defense. "What about Dallas?" he asked, careful to keep his voice at low modulation.

"I told you that wouldn't work," she proclaimed.

■ ■ ■ ■

The next morning at eleven, Emily took off from work, helped check him out of the hospital, and drove him home to his red door and town house on Nineteenth Street.

"That red door works for you now, Hugo," said Emily as they entered. "It didn't before."

Hugo held his tongue. Easy. Ease her out of his life — out of this picture.

Once he was situated inside, she said, "I'm going to stop by my place for some things, and I'll be back this evening. If you're up to it, we could walk over to Connecticut for a bite."

It was a declaration, not a question.

He wondered — in vain and only partly in jest — how he might possibly disappear without a trace before she returned.

The important matter was how much he treasured being back in his house. The sights and smells of where and how he lived made him feel good. But after a few moments, he was hit for the first time with the real downside of what had happened to him at the courthouse.

His cleaning lady had stacked the mail neatly on the hall table. On top of it she had left him a note: "I so proud work for you. Andrea."

Underneath was an invitation-size envelope that was made of heavy, expensive white paper. MR. HUGO MARDER was on the front, with no address and no stamp. It had obviously been hand-delivered.

Hugo opened it and removed a notecard with the words HOUSE ON THE KLONG engraved in simple red ink at the top.

Below in small, precise handwriting was the message:

Dear Mr. Marder,

I would consider it a privilege of unsurpassed glory to mount a feast at my restaurant in your honor. You decide on the date and the guests and I will, with pleasure, do the rest.

This is an offer, sir, that will never expire as long as the both of us are allowed to breathe the air of life into our lungs and the joy of celebration into our souls.

Your admiring servant,
You Johnny

Below his signature, You Johnny had scrawled, "No bear claw soup will be served. I promise."

There was a small U.S. Mail Eagle box underneath the note. Hugo glanced at the return address. He knew it was a pair of cuff links made from old Detroit bus tokens he had bought three weeks ago from a fellow collector in Cleveland. The rest of the mail were bills, solicitations. Nothing much personal.

He went to his computer. Nothing much personal here, either. The week's collection of 101 e-mails was mostly spam: offers to refinance his home, buy drugs without a doctor's prescription, and enlarge the size of his penis. He was sick of cleaning this garbage out of his e-mail in-box every day. When was the government going to do something about spam? Why did they call it spam, anyhow?

His answering machine was also chock-full of messages. Some were from local newspeople wanting comments or photographs. Most were from strangers who had called to congratulate him. Again, nothing much personal other than calls from Robert, Jackson Dyer, and a few others at the store repeating for the record what they had already said in notes and calls to the hospital.

The mail, the e-mail, the phone messages. Nothing much personal. Hugo was struck with what that said about his life — the *old* one. Who in the hell would he even invite to You Johnny's celebratory feast? He had made and nurtured no close friends since Emily left him. Robert was a work friend but not that close — not, until recently, even very personal. Who else was there? The socializing he did when married had always been within Emily's work circle and demeaning and miserable for Hugo.

In Dallas, Hugo hereby vowed, he would mount a major effort to make friends — to be a friend. His goal would be to have enough friends to eventually fill a Dallas restaurant the size of the House on the Klong and then some.

# Eight

Hugo arrived at the back entrance, through which he had passed so many times over the last seventeen years. His wristwatch said it was 9:42. That was a surprise. Normally, this walk took only twenty-five minutes, but this morning it had been seven minutes longer.

His heavy thoughts, obviously, had made his steps heavier and slower.

Much of what he had been thinking had to do with Emily. He had told her that he was going to be entertaining "a lady visitor" for dinner the night before, a ploy just to keep her away from him. To back up his lie, Hugo had gone to a Chinese take-out place. He bought enough for two, took it home, divided it equally on two plates, ate most everything on one, and put the other plateful down the disposal. He was careful to put both dirty plates and matching pairs of silverware and glasses into the dishwasher.

Emily was one of those people who noticed things.

Hugo was already in his bed, and almost asleep, when she arrived just after ten o'clock. After she called upstairs, he listened while she locked up and, yes, rustled around in the kitchen. He heard the dishwasher being opened and, a few seconds later, closed. He also thought she may have checked the trash can for signs of some kind of brought-in food. He knew Emily.

She came into his room carrying a small green canvas duffel he recognized.

"When did she leave?" she asked almost immediately.

"An hour or so ago."

"How do you feel?"

"Tired — but otherwise, fine."

"Did you have sex with her?"

Hugo felt the warmth shoot into his face. "God, no."

"I think I smell it in here."

"You're imagining things," he said, assuming his face was now as red as his front door.

"Do you want me to give you a quick one now?"

"No. But thanks. I'm really bushed. Thanks." *Jesus!*

To his further alarm, she started taking off her clothes.

"Hey, you know, Emily, it might be best for you to sleep in the guest room. I think with this shoulder, that would be best. Wouldn't want a swinging arm or leg to knock loose some stitches or anything like that." Easy does it.

"Fine," she said, picking up her duffel and disappearing through the door.

In the morning, she was up, dressed, and on her way out for work by seven-thirty. She came into the bedroom only to say, "I'll be home about seven. Have a restful day. Planning anything?"

"I'm going over to the store later this morning to talk to Jackson," he said. "I called yesterday afternoon and told him I would."

"I think it's time you started to think of something other than Nash Brothers. That doesn't quite work for the New Hugo."

And she was gone, leaving Hugo uncertain, as he walked to the store, if easy-does-it was going to get the job done with her.

That led to further what-ifs and what-nexts if he should be exposed — unmasked. Could he really spend the rest of his life wondering if the next phone call was from a reporter or somebody threatening to tell the world what he really was?

He opened the door to the store.

For Hugo's a jolly good fellow,
For Hugo's a jolly good fellow,
For Hugo's a jolly good fe-ell-low . . .
That nobody can deny!

There they all were. Jackson, Robert, the whole floor, as well as the administrative and tailoring and shipping and janitorial team. All twenty-six of the people who made Nash Brothers what it was here on L Street, Northwest, in Washington, D.C. They were standing in a semicircle below a large handmade banner that had been taped high up on the wall. It was a long strip of white Nash Brothers wrapping paper with HUGO, OUR HERO written across it in large black letters.

There was applause. There were a few shouts and whistles.

Hugo's first thought was that if he was going to be exposed, he wished it would have happened before this. How could he ever again show his face to any of these colleagues?

Jackson stepped forward and shook Hugo's hand with both of his. "Everyone at headquarters in New York said to tell you how proud they are of you, too," he said.

Larry Stuart, a shirt-sweater-tie man, gently slapped Hugo on the back — the left side. Everyone clearly knew Hugo had been shot in the right shoulder and could see that he was favoring it as he walked in. "I never had the foggiest notion that you were a marine, Hugo. Why didn't you tell us?"

"Yeah, yeah," said Bill J. Koker, a suit-sport coat man, like Hugo. "Hugo Marder, the bashful hero. Boy, that sounded like some hot time you had at the courthouse. Congratulations, my friend." Friend? Bill and Hugo worked well together, but Hugo never thought of him as a friend. Hugo always found Koker a bit standoffish, cold. They had never once spoken in personal terms. But now Hugo was "my friend."

"Why didn't you ever wear that Silver Star pin here at work?" asked Guy Dean, the chief bookkeeper, pointing to Hugo's coat lapel. Hugo had considered wearing the red and white pin that went with his District Medal of Honor, but then he realized he had to wear the Silver Star this morning. "We'd have loved to know you were a marine hero, Hugo."

Lee Chau Lui, one of the tailors, said, "I am most impressed with you, Mr. Hugo Marder. There are so few heroes in our lives."

They all gathered around him. Somebody said it was the proudest day of his life at Nash Brothers. Another wondered if Hugo would sign the *Herald* story for his son.

At first Hugo managed only to fake smiles and laughs and much humility. But soon he was genuinely happy. He couldn't help himself. Yes, he was an undeserving Silver Star impostor, but he really had taken action at the courthouse and, most important, he had never in his life had a group of peers — of any kind of people — treat him, admire him, like this.

Never in his life had he been considered a person who was special.

As the clock over the store entrance struck ten and Jackson Dyer went to unlock the front door, the staff scattered to their sales posts.

Robert stayed by Hugo's side.

"Your whole being seemed to shine like the brightest of suns just now," said Robert, the only person in the room who knew the truth about Ron Derby Cunningham's Silver Star and the marines. "I have never before, not even at high moments in my own very emotional country, witnessed a man experiencing exquisite joy the way you did with all of us, Hugo."

As usual, Robert had read Hugo's situation absolutely right. Hugo said, "I had no idea such a feeling was possible."

Robert said, "It proves only that you have lived a life that was too calm, dear Sir Hugo."

"But now I am living another man's life, not mine. It's great while it lasts, but who knows how long that will be."

"To repeat one of my earlier truths: You can make it last forever, if you wish."

Hugo didn't believe that for a second. But he said nothing.

Robert said he had to go. A See You was coming in at ten-fifteen. "He's a gentleman who comes in once every two years and buys six, sometimes seven, pairs of different styles of Ballys. I must not disappoint him."

Though Hugo understood, he wanted to say something else to Robert, something about building on their friendship, maybe getting to know his wife and two teenage sons.

But Robert left, and Jackson came in from the sales floor.

"You wanted to talk to me, Hugo?" he said, motioning for Hugo to go first toward his office.

"I want to explore the possibility of transferring to the store in Dallas," said Hugo.

A look of disblief and dismay came over Jackson's face. "You suddenly become a public hero, which transforms you into a magnet that will suck customers into our store in a way we have never seen. And you want to leave it all and go to Dallas?"

Hugo nodded and then looked away.

"Why, Hugo?"

"To tell you the truth, I need to get away. They won't know about me in Dallas, I can freshen up my life, recover from all of this mental as well as the physical . . ." Hugo shifted his shoulder and winced.

Jackson leaned across the desk where they were seated. "Oh my God, yes. I understand, Hugo. Forgive me. You have been through quite an ordeal. I hadn't thought about the head stuff. You bet, I definitely understand. I will get right on your request. I can't imagine anyone at Nash Brothers saying no to you about anything right now."

Hugo smiled.

"But why Dallas?" Jackson asked. "I never heard of anybody moving to Dallas."

Hugo repeated lamely what he had said to Emily about the museums and the weather. Then he rose to leave. "I don't want to keep you any longer," he said.

But Jackson motioned him back down. He wanted a personal account of what had happened in the jury room. Hugo went through it, and when he'd finished, Jackson snapped his fingers. "Hugo, I also forgot to give you this." He handed Hugo an oversize white business envelope. "Mr. Andrews himself dropped this off, saying to give it to you when you came back to the store."

Hugo took the envelope and left.

Walking home as fast as he ever had, he carried it in his left hand down by his side, barely allowing it to move or swing with his step, as if it were a letter bomb — an explosive.

The moment he was behind the red door, he opened the envelope. It was unsealed. Inside was another, smaller one that was sealed.

The return address in the upper-left corner said: "The Department of Defense — Office of the Assistant Secretary for Personnel."

"The Honorable Dalton T. Andrews" was handwritten in black pen across the front, as was "Confidential" in the lower-right corner and "By Hand" in the lower left.

A handwritten note from Mr. Andrews was clipped to it.

Hugo — I thought you might want the official record for your scrapbook. Again, congratulations. Dalton Andrews

Hugo went into the den, grabbed a metal letter opener, and slit open the flap. Inside was a letter.

Dear Mr. Andrews:
I regret to report that the search of Department of Defense files for the information you requested has not been successful. No one by the name of Hugo Colin Marder, or any related initials or names combination, was awarded the Silver Star medal for gallantry in action during the Vietnam War. An expanded search revealed that no one by that name has ever received any medal for heroism in any war. The records also failed to confirm that someone by that name was ever inducted into or served in the U.S. Marine Corps at any rank at any time.

A person by the name of Hugo Colin Marder did turn up in the files of the Selective Service System. It showed that he was registered for the draft in the 1960s but was never called to serve. He was deferred by his draft board in Newton, Michigan, on two different occasions because of a college deferment.

If there is anything else we may do,

please let us know.

Sincerely,
Owen S. Moberly
Assistant Secretary for Personnel

Since the envelope was still sealed, did that mean Mr. Andrews had not read it? *Yes!* That also explained his cover note. Mr. Andrews never would have scribbled "congratulations" to a fraudulent hero. He must have forwarded the letter on without even opening it.

Hugo began preparations for his new life in Dallas, Texas, going at the research with the same vigor and determination with which he had transformed himself into a former marine. This task would be much easier, of course. He was only going to live in Texas, not be a Texan. That would be one more transformation than he was up to.

Transformation. Quite a word. He realized he was now way, *way* beyond wanting people to think he was a former marine hero who had won the Silver Star. He'd been transformed into an entirely different person . . . a stronger person.

Whatever, he was going to Dallas to be who he was now.

At his computer, he simply typed "Dallas,

Texas" into Google's search window and went to work.

He immediately found the website for the Dallas Convention & Visitors Bureau. "Welcome to Dallas," it proclaimed. "Thank you," Hugo said back to the computer screen. Then he browsed through the site's various offerings, which included a rundown of coming cultural and entertainment events, as well as constant reminders that Dallas had a professional football team called the Cowboys and a history that included the 1963 assassination of President John F. Kennedy. There was even a Dallas song called "Big D," from a 1956 musical, *The Most Happy Fella.* He recalled the old Hit Parade song "I've Got a Gal in Kalamazoo," which had been popular in Newton, thirty miles away, when he was growing up.

The major find was dallasnews.com, the website of *The Dallas Morning News,* Dallas's only daily newspaper. Hugo registered and then clicked all the right places to receive an e-mailed shorthand version of the paper every day. The site even had the classified ads, regular weather updates, lottery results, traffic reports, and most everything anyone would ever need to know about Dallas. And it was completely free.

*The Washington Post* and *The New York Times* had similar operations, which had already made Hugo wonder how newspapers could afford to give away on the Internet what they were charging for with their own print version. Hugo figured the papers' owners must know what they were doing. The important thing for him was that he was able — beginning right now — to automatically bring Dallas into his life every morning.

From the *News* classifieds and several other places, he put together a list of rental agents and properties that, according to a map, would place him within a reasonable walking distance to the Nash Brothers store at NorthPark.

Then he located hotels and motels in the NorthPark area, as well as a cheap Washington–Dallas round-trip airfare and rental-car special.

Next weekend, Emily and all other potentially awful things permitting, Hugo would make his first trip to Dallas. He would go, as they say in the marines, to reconnoiter the terrain and situation of his better life.

Before leaving the dallasnews.com website, he scanned through its "recent news" archives for possible mentions of his courthouse heroics. There was only one — a three-paragraph story that had run on page seven of the *News* the day after.

Emily was carrying take-out spaghetti and meatballs when she came into Hugo's house after work. Hugo saw it as a pointed follow-up to his phantom date the night before.

"I know it's one of your favorites," she said, setting the small kitchen table for two.

Hugo had made no preparations for the evening, except maybe to take Emily to dinner at one of the places over on Connecticut. It was true that he had always loved spaghetti and meatballs, a taste that came from those made by his aunt Lily. (She mixed sausage in with the ground meat and put sugar in the tomato sauce.) But the South Beach diet prohibited pasta, so he hadn't had any in weeks.

He figured he could eat the meatballs and maybe a couple of bites of the pasta and scatter the rest around his plate. But that didn't matter. It wasn't the food he would chew tonight with Emily that was important; it was the words.

"I talked to Jackson today about a transfer," he said after they were seated at the table.

"I didn't know there was another Nash

Brothers store around here. Where is it, Tysons Corner — or White Flint Mall?"

Hugo couldn't tell whether she was playing with him or she really had forgotten what he'd said about moving to Dallas. He never had been good at separating out this kind of thing with Emily.

"Dallas, Emily," he said, in a quiet version of his new marine way of talking. "I'm transferring to the store in Dallas. Jackson said it would be no problem, he was sure. It's essentially a done deal, as you political people say."

Emily took a long gulp of red wine, a semi-cheap merlot he had opened. "Are you asking me to go with you?" she said, looking right at him.

"Do you want to go?"

"That wasn't the question."

"That's the answer."

" 'No,' then, is your answer. You don't want me to go."

Hugo — the *new* Hugo — didn't look away. "I repeat — do you want to go?"

"I already told you, Dallas doesn't work for . . . well, me."

"It does for me."

"So you don't want to remarry?"

He took a deep mental breath. "Not if you won't go to Dallas."

"I won't."

"What sense, then, would it make to re-marry?"

"None at all."

In silence, she downed the last of her wine, took one more bite of her dinner, wiped her mouth with a napkin, and shoved her chair back. "So I'm gone again, Hugo."

In what seemed like less than two minutes, she had cleaned her place at the table, stuck the dirty dishes and silverware in the dishwasher, gone upstairs, and returned with her small duffel.

Hugo had remained at the table, continuing to drink his wine and appear to eat his spaghetti while mostly thinking about whether she might now expose him as a phony marine.

"Shakespeare was wrong, wasn't he?" Emily said, standing in the doorway between the kitchen and the entrance hall, ready to go.

"About what?" Hugo asked.

"When he said parting is such sweet sorrow. It wasn't the first time for us, and it isn't now."

Hugo, uneasy about what she was up to, chose to ignore the issue of Shakespeare.

Then she came over to him and brushed his forehead with a kiss. "I will leave you alone to be and do whatever the hell you want," she said. "And in case you're wondering, our deal holds."

He was wondering, all right. "Thanks."

At the doorway, she said, "For the record, Hugo, if you had asked me to go to Dallas with you and really meant it, I might — *might* — have gone."

That, of course, was precisely what Hugo had feared.

"Except for your pointless, stupid shortsightedness in staying with Nash Brothers," she added, "you're beginning to turn out to be the man I thought I'd married."

That, too, was precisely what Hugo had feared — and hoped.

NorthPark was a most elegant shopping center. It was completely enclosed, with valet parking, a variety of outdoor sculpture and other art amid Neiman Marcus, Foley's, Dillard's, and Lord & Taylor department stores, scores of restaurants, and the other of its 120 or so establishments.

Nash Brothers, about the same size as the store in Washington, was on the lower level.

"Hugo Marder, it's a pleasure," said the manager. "I'm P. J. Rodriguez." A sales associate at the door had summoned the manager after Hugo introduced himself.

At a glance, if there was an exact opposite to Jackson Dyer, P. J. Rodriguez was it.

First off, she was a woman. P.J., it turned out, stood for Priscilla Jan. She was Hispanic. Also, she was absolutely gorgeous to look at and, in her early forties, ten years younger than Jackson.

Those differences were only the physical basics.

Meeting her for the first time presented Hugo with a whiplashing mix of instant reactions.

A woman manager of a *men's* clothing store! Affirmative action run amok?

Then he remembered that some Nash Brothers stores had begun introducing new lines of women's clothes, mostly from Armani, Polo, and DKNY. Washington was not one of those stores, but there were rumors it was coming. It had already happened here at the Dallas store.

A Latina! Affirmative action run amok to a second power?

In his seventeen years selling clothes, Hugo could not remember one Latino customer. There may have been a few foreign diplomats from Latin America, but that was it. Then he remembered that Dallas was in Texas. There were a lot of Latinos in Texas.

Such a beautiful woman! How could male sales associates concentrate on business with her around?

On second thought: Maybe, just maybe, this was an extraordinarily special perk of working — or shopping — in this particular store. What's the problem with having a stunningly beautiful woman to gaze upon between customers?

But so young! Managers should be experienced, seasoned professionals, people who have sold millions of dollars' worth of quality Nash Brothers merchandise to quality customers. . . .

On their walk through the floor, Hugo's attention had been mostly — he couldn't help it — on her long black hair, which fell straight to just below her shoulders; her back, her butt, and her legs, all of which seemed perfectly formed and moved in a gentle synchronization as she glided ahead of him toward her office in the rear of the store. She was wearing a beige silk suit that Hugo could only assume came from the store. The same rules must apply for female staff — wear only Nash Brothers clothes and wear them well.

When he sat down across a desk from her, he was able to focus on her face. The skin, a light brown olive, was smooth, silky, almost shiny. But there was some slight crow's-feet cracking around the eyelids, which encircled the two most glistening black eyes Hugo had ever seen. He couldn't take his own eyes off of them. Maybe she was older than he at first thought. Maybe she really was experienced enough to be a manager.

"I'll bet I can guess what's going through your mind right now," she said.

Wrong! At least Hugo hoped to hell she was wrong. Because if she really could read the faintest lust that was in him at this moment, she would follow that realization by instantly booting him out of a job at this store before he even began.

When he only smiled, she said, " 'Hey, what's a woman doing managing a Nash Brothers store?' Did I guess right?" Her voice was soft but firm. She could have been a woman marine. Semper Fi, P.J.!

"No, no," Hugo said.

"I hope you weren't misled by my name," she said.

He really had been. Less than a week after talking to Jackson, Hugo had received a most cordial letter from the Dallas manager, expressing delight at the prospect of his "joining our Dallas team." Jackson had made the follow-up phone call to arrange

Hugo's visit to the store.

Jackson must have known P. J. Rodriguez was a woman. The phone call aside, there were regular national sales and merchandise introduction meetings that involved all store managers. Would Jackson have withheld the information intentionally, thinking Hugo might not want to work under a woman? No, no. Could it be that Jackson simply didn't think it was important enough to mention? Why would he think it would be a problem for Hugo — or anybody else? Yes. That must have been it.

"Oh, no, certainly not," Hugo gushed in answer to her question. "It wouldn't have mattered anyhow."

"That's good to hear," said P.J. with a smile that was pleasant but more professional than personal. "I've been told there are some veteran sales associates in the older stores, particularly in the East, who would probably have severe adjustment problems."

"I'm not one of those," Hugo said. And as he said it, he felt he was telling a lie. He was overcome with the vague thought that he was going to have trouble working in Dallas for P. J. Rodriguez. Not because she was a woman, Hispanic, and distractingly beautiful. There was something else, maybe just a hunch, an impression. Something in her letter came back to him: "I am sure you will immediately be made to feel at home by our staff, most especially the twenty-three sales associates who will be your new colleagues. One in particular, I am sure, will be most special to you. I will let that be a surprise."

P. J. Rodriguez broke into another smile, aimed not at Hugo but over his left shoulder, at a person behind him.

"Yes, Phil, here he is," she said, standing. "Come in and meet Hugo Marder."

Hugo turned in his chair. It was a man, about Hugo's height and age. He was all aglow as he approached with his right hand extended.

"What a treat," said the man as he shook Hugo's hand. "I have been so looking forward to this."

"Thank you, thank you," Hugo said.

"I'm Phil Cacivio," said the man. "Welcome to Dallas and to this store — and to boot camp under the one, the only, P. J. Rodriguez."

Hugo glanced back at P.J. She was grinning with enjoyment. This was all okay with her.

Hugo took a closer look at Phil Cacivio. His black hair was short, and he was dressed, much like Hugo, in a Nash Brothers dark blue slight-stripe suit, a white European-collar shirt, and a gleaming, soft red-cream-and-blue-patterned tie.

Then he saw it. There in the left lapel of Cacivio's suit was a blue and white Navy Cross pin.

"Semper Fi, Lieutenant," said Cacivio. "My serial number was oh-eight-nine-four-five-seven."

Hugo went numb. And then quickly to the ready.

Phil, with P.J.'s warm and enthusiastic encouragement, insisted that he take Hugo to lunch after "a trip through Rodriguez-land."

He escorted Hugo to every department of the store and introduced him to every sales associate working this Saturday.

None of it registered with Hugo. Not the way the departments — men's suits and sport coats in the back, shirts here, shoes there, ties and accessories up front, the new women's section on the left, and so on — were arranged and outfitted. Not the faces, names, ages, gender, or races of the people who would be his new colleagues.

Hugo was thinking about what he was going to do and say at lunch. Would this be the beginning of his New Life or the end of it?

The restaurant was a huge Chicago-in-the-twenties Italian place on the upper level of the mall, less than a ten-minute walk from Nash Brothers. As they entered, Phil was talking about the wonderfulness of working in an environment here at North-Park that matched the tasteful ambience of Nash Brothers.

Once seated across from Phil at a corner table, Hugo ordered veal parmigiana with a caprese salad — mozzarella and sliced tomatoes with olive oil. There was a life-size blow-up of Al Capone's Chicago mug shot on the wall directly behind Phil.

Hugo made eye contact with Al and imagined it could be John Wayne instead.

To avoid exposure, Hugo had to learn enough about each piece of Phil's marine chronology and experience before revealing anything about his own.

"So, when were you in the Corps?" he asked Phil the second the waiter left their table.

"Sixty-five to sixty-nine," said Phil. "You?"

"Sixty-three to sixty-seven."

Having eliminated a potential Basic School problem, Hugo asked, "Why the marines?"

"It was a family thing. My dad and two uncles had been marines. It's in the blood. We're Italians, and we're marines."

"I was the first marine in my family. It was a childhood-dream thing. You a PLC?"

"NROTC."

"I was PLC. What outfit in Vietnam?"

"The Sixth Marines."

Great! "What battalion?"

"Twenty-third . . . most of the time but not all. How about you?"

"I was in the Ninth Marines. One-Nine."

"The Walking Dead. You poor bastards really caught it."

"I was one of the lucky ones. Where did you get that?" Hugo nodded at Phil's Navy Cross lapel pin.

"Near Khe Sanh."

"Doing what?"

"I'm not keen on going into all of that anymore. What about you and your Silver Star?"

"I feel the same way."

Their first courses came, and Hugo, with relief, went after his caprese. He decided the worst was over, at least for now.

The conversation moved on to an exchange of non-marine personal histories. Hugo, in line with his new make-friends mode, offered all of his own details and pressed Phil for his.

Phil had grown up in Oklahoma. His hometown was north of Tulsa, where his family had moved from northern Italy after World War II and a long stopover in Chicago. His father had been a marine enlisted man in the war and then had taken a job with Phillips 66, an oil company headquartered in Oklahoma. Phil went to the University of Oklahoma at Norman on a naval ROTC scholarship and, on graduation, took the marine option and was commissioned a marine second lieutenant. He met his wife, Anne, at O.U. Still married, they had two children, a boy of seventeen and a girl of fourteen, and lived in the Dallas suburb of Plano.

"That's right out the east doors of North-Park and onto the North Central Expressway for fifteen miles," Phil said.

"An easy commute?" Hugo asked.

"Only when it's not rush hour, and it seems sometimes like it never is not rush hour on Central. I'm in my car at least forty-five minutes each way, every day. You given any thought to where you're going to live?"

Hugo said he was going to look at some apartments and town houses this afternoon. "Someplace close enough to NorthPark so I can walk to work, like I've done in Washington every day for seventeen years. I don't own a car anymore — Emily took it." When telling Phil his own personal story, Hugo had named Emily as his former — and only — wife.

An incredulous smile broke across Phil's face. "You can't live in Dallas without a car, Hugo. It's impossible. I mean, impossible."

Phil said Dallas was a great place, but everything was spread out, and public transportation and even sidewalks were too scarce to manage a life on your feet instead of wheels.

Hugo's budget did not include a car. But, he figured, one thing at a time. Find a place to live, get settled there and at the store, and then take his time shaking out the rest.

His veal parmigiana came. The portion was huge, too much for his low-carb diet, but he consumed it with the same passion he had the caprese. Things were going well with Phil, why not eat up?

Phil dug into an even larger plate of spaghetti and meatballs.

Looking over at it, Hugo said, "Sure beats the hell out of S.O.S., doesn't it?"

Phil said nothing. His face showed no recognition of what Hugo was talking about.

"S.O.S. You know, shit on a shingle,"

Hugo persisted.

Phil broke into a smile. "Oh my God, yes. I had completely put that out of my mind."

They talked about the store. Phil said the working atmosphere and relationships were really good. There was a cooperative spirit. Nobody had sharp elbows or violated the See You and Call rules. He acknowledged that North Dallas was the most prosperous part of Dallas, and NorthPark was the best, largest, and busiest shopping center. As a consequence, there was plenty of business for every sales associate.

"Why did you go to work for Nash Brothers?" Hugo asked. It came out casually, but he could see Phil flick his eyes and then look away. The question, for some reason, had made him uncomfortable. At first Hugo didn't get it, but then he thought maybe there was too much of a "What's a former marine Navy Cross hero doing selling clothes?" inference to it.

Whatever, Hugo quickly moved on. "*I* did because I couldn't find a job doing what I really wanted to do, which was be in graphics, a cartoonist — really. When I was a kid, I never dreamed of someday selling men's clothes."

"Me, neither," said Phil. And that was all he said.

Hugo asked about P. J. Rodriguez.

"She's a beauty in every way, Hugo," Phil said, clearly grateful for a new subject; particularly, it seemed, P. J. Rodriguez. "You'll fall in love with her, like all the rest of us."

Hugo refrained from saying that he already had.

Phil, speaking softly and with respect, told P.J.'s story of being a Nash Brothers legacy employee.

"Her dad, a kid from Puerto Rico, went to work for the main New York store when he was seventeen, as a cleanup boy," said Phil. "He advanced to tailor's assistant, tailor trainee, tailor, and, finally, chief tailor."

He and his wife had two children, P.J. and a son named Manuel. The father wanted more than anything for his son to become a Nash Brothers sales associate, which to him was the ultimate achievment.

"Manuel was all lined up to do that when Vietnam came along. He was drafted, went into the army and to Vietnam, and was blown to bits by a land mine. To give solace to a heartbroken father, P.J., then still called Priscilla, took her brother's place."

P. J. Rodriguez thus became Nash Brothers' first woman sales associate, hired as a

224

special case — because of her father — long before there was even a thought of selling women's clothes.

As Phil spoke with increasing pleasure, Hugo's crush on P. J. Rodriguez bloomed and deepened.

Said Phil, "She was a great salesperson. I mean *great* great. She accepted the Dallas job five years ago — just before I came, in fact. That made her the first woman manager in the history of Nash Brothers. She's been a first at just about everything she's done in life."

Hugo thought he saw traces of moisture in Phil's eyes. He hadn't taken a bite while he told the story. Neither had Hugo.

Clearly, Phil Cacivio was a long way from being over falling in love with Priscilla Jan Rodriguez.

It had been a long lunch, nearly two hours. Phil picked up the check, assuring Hugo, "P.J. said this one was definitely on the store."

Hugo felt for the first time that special bonding that seems to exist between all marines. It was the kind of thing Lane, Buchwald, and Russell had spoken of so eloquently and thankfully at the Smithsonian.

Maybe, in this Italian restaurant in Dallas,

Hugo had moved beyond the Crucible? Maybe he was no longer just acting like a marine, he was feeling it?

"I'm really looking forward to working with you, Phil," Hugo said once they were outside the restaurant and in the mall. He was heading to his rental car and an afternoon of housing hunting; Phil was going back to work. "The marine experience is truly important, isn't it?"

"It certainly is," Phil said. "There aren't many of us in Dallas — and the few there are were mostly aviators from the air station over at Grand Prairie."

"I assume you were infantry."

"You bet. What was it called — the infantry MOS. Oh-four?"

"Oh-three, actually." Hugo knew from *The Marine Officer's Guide* that there was no 04 MOS.

"Right. That's what I was. An oh-three. How easy we forget that stuff."

What was it Matt Columbia had said about marines and their MOS?

Oh my God.

"Semper Fi, Hugo," Phil said as they parted.

"Semper Fi, Phil."

The next few hours remained with Hugo

afterward mostly as a blur.

In rapid-fire order, he inspected more than a dozen different apartments and town houses. Some were with one of two agents with whom he had made appointments via their websites; the rest he did on his own, simply showing up and asking to see the vacancy. But when he was finished and it was almost dark and he was driving back to his motel across the expressway from North-Park, he could remember little of what he had seen and done.

His obsessive thoughts during his touring were overpoweringly on Phil Cacivio, not on matters involving bedroom sizes, washer-dryer combinations, off-street parking, or free health club memberships.

More than once, the thoughts burst to the surface. While peering into some kind of refrigerator in some kind of kitchen or a walk-in closet in a bedroom, he would start laughing. The person with him, whether an agent or an apartment manager, would be both startled and annoyed.

Hugo always apologized but never explained. How could he tell them that his guffaw had been prompted by the possibility that there were two phony former marines, each about the same age, each posing as a hero by wearing a medal lapel pin he did not win, each claiming to have served as an infantry officer in Vietnam, and now — believe it or not — each about to work as a sales associate in the same Nash Brothers store in the NorthPark Center in Dallas, Texas.

Over and over, Hugo told himself this simply could not be. Phil had to be real. Then he remembered what Mr. Andrews had said about how widespread this "sickness" was among men.

Over and over, Hugo went through the evidence.

— Phil clearly did not know anything about shit on a shingle.

— He evaded the specifics of his Vietnam service and his Navy Cross.

— He said his MOS was 04.

On the other hand:

— He recited a serial number.

— He knew the difference between PLC and NROTC.

— He *did* know about the Ninth Marines

and said it right.

— He knew One-Nine was called the Walking Dead.

Hugo thought about little else while eating a room-service cheeseburger without the bun, while watching one cop show after another on television, and then while spending the rest of the night in a vain attempt to get some peaceful sleep.

His turmoil was still right there with him when he got up in the morning and drove back to the Dallas–Fort Worth Airport for the flight back to Washington.

# NINE

Minutes after passing through his red door, he had the information he wanted about Phil Cacivio.

Mr. Andrews had been correct. Information about medal winners was available on the Internet. Hugo found a website that listed the names, ranks, and outfits of the 361 marines who had been awarded the Navy Cross in Vietnam.

There he was. "Cacivio, Phillip J.— 1Lt.— Feb. 7, 1968 — B 3/26 (1st Mar Div)."

Hugo clicked on the "Citation" box and the following document, similar to Ron Cunningham's Silver Star account, came on the screen:

The President of the United States takes pride in presenting the NAVY CROSS to:

**First Lieutenant Phillip J. Cacivio**
**United States Marine Corps**

## For service as set forth
## in the following:

CITATION

For extraordinary heroism on 7 February 1968 while Platoon Commander of Company B, Third Battalion, 26th Marines, First Division, in connection with combat operations against enemy forces in the Republic of Vietnam. After leading a relief force to aid a combat patrol that had sustained heavy casualties, including its platoon sergeant leader, First Lieutenant Cacivio led his unit through concentrated enemy mortar and automatic weapons fire. Three of his own men were wounded near a hostile machine gun. With enemy soldiers firing directly at him, he threw three grenades into the enemy gun emplacement, destroying the gun and the soldiers manning it. He was trying to administer first aid to his own men when fire from another enemy position pinned him down and a grenade landed near his fallen men. First Lieutenant Cacivio kicked the grenade aside and threw himself between it and the casualties to protect them from the explosion. Still under fire, and even though fragments from the grenade caused a painful wound to his left leg, he rallied his Marines, grabbed the radio from his critically wounded radio operator, and restored communications. After radioing his unit's location, he used his hands and a small machete to slash a path to a helicopter landing zone, returned to the casualties, and carried three of his men, one after another, back for evacuation. He continued to direct the operation until his own blood loss made it impossible for him to continue and he was also evacuated to a medical facility. By his indomitable courage, determined fighting spirit, and selfless devotion to duty, First Lieutenant Cacivio was directly instrumental in saving the lives of several of his fellow Marines, thereby upholding the highest traditions of the Marine Corps and the United States Naval Service.

For the President<br>The Secretary of the Navy

Hugo read it once silently. Then he did so again, out loud.

On impulse, he hit a TODAY's MARINE NEWS link on the website.

Up came a story from a newspaper in McAllen, Texas, about a twenty-two-year-old marine named Raymundo J. Garza who had been killed in Iraq. He had been president of the McAllen High School student body and played quarterback on the football team. As an honor student, he was awarded a congressional appointment to the Naval Academy at Annapolis and commissioned a marine second lieutenant. He was commanding an infantry platoon in the First Marine Division when it came under heavy fire in Al Anbar Province in Iraq.

"Lieutenant Garza was hit by a rocket propelled grenade as he exposed himself to enemy fire rallying his platoon.

"He will be buried with full military honors at South City Cemetery following a mass at St. Xavier Catholic Church, McAllen, at 2 P.M. Thursday. Classmates and fellow football team members from his high school class will be honorary pallbearers. His former coach as well as his older brother and his uncle, an assistant county clerk, will speak. The Right Reverend Alonzo Torrez, archbishop of the Harlingen diocese, will officiate.

"Bishop Torrez was the priest at St. Xavier when Lieutenant Garza was an altar boy there . . ."

Next to the story was a large color portrait of a young man in a white marine officer's hat with a gold and silver globe/anchor marine emblem in the center.

The late lieutenant Garza had a steady, proud look on his light brown face and in his pitch-black eyes.

"Family members said Marine officers told them Lieutenant Garza's Marine comrades had recommended him to receive a posthumous Navy Cross or a Silver Star for his bravery," the newspaper story concluded.

Hugo's eyes filled with tears.

He clicked on another dead marine's story. A nineteen-year-old PFC named Winslow from Brooklyn had died from a sniper's bullet. Then another — a twenty-seven-year-old captain, a company commander, had been killed in a mortar attack. A corporal, twenty, had been killed when his Humvee ran over a land mine.

And another and another. Real marines. Real marines who had learned the walk and the talk and had their heads shaved and lived real stories.

From his computer, Hugo ran to the hall closet, feverishly removed the Silver Star case, and thrust the lapel pin back in its proper place with the medal and ribbon.

The case firmly in hand, he raced out the door and trotted toward Connecticut Avenue.

There, he headed north.

He paused briefly at the House on the Klong.

Then he kept moving on up the hill on the east sidewalk, alternating between a sprint and a vigorous walk, past the Washington Hilton, General McClellan, a mansion now used by the Russian Federation's trade delegation, a much smaller town house that was Malta's embassy, and three stately apartment buildings.

He crossed the street in front of the Chinese embassy and continued due north to pass by the imperial lion on the left entrance of William Howard Taft Bridge.

Hugo halted near the midpoint in the three-hundred-yard bridge and moved two long steps back from the railing to the curb.

He jerked his right hand back behind him like a baseball pitcher. There was a shot of pain from his shoulder wound, but it didn't matter. He sucked in a huge gush of air.

Then he brought his fully extended arm up over his head and hurled the case with Ron Derby Cunningham's Silver Star high and far into the air with more strength than he had ever summoned in his life.

Hugo Marder's days as a phony marine were over.

You Johnny said there was no need to place an order with a waiter. The food and drink would simply continue arriving until the evening ended, if it ever did. "There is no requirement that it should do so," he said.

There was joy in his pronouncement, which he made as Hugo and his invited guests assembled in the Chiang Mai Room, a private dining room on the second floor of the House on the Klong. You Johnny said Chiang Mai was a beautiful resort city in northwest Thailand that was famous for its elephants. That explained why the ceilings were covered with gold line drawings of elephants, the walls were crowded with elephant paintings, the white linen place mats and napkins were marked with orange embroidered elephants, the china and glassware were decorated with small blue elephants, and the salt and pepper shakers were miniature yellow or red elephants.

The large round dining table was already overflowing with platters of appetizers — vegetable and salmon rolls, bits of chicken on small sticks, shrimp and crabmeat dumplings, and a number of other Thai dishes, mostly fish, that were not familiar to Hugo. There were also a variety of Asian beers on ice and uncorked bottles of champagne and white wine with three young Thai men in black pants and white shirts to answer every need.

Hugo accepted a glass of champagne and took a large, long first gulp.

All the elements of a true night to remember were in place. He had no doubt that *he* would remember it, but in much the same way as those who attended the Last Supper.

Hugo had spent the four days since Taft Bridge arranging himself for this dinner.

The easy part was You Johnny, who seemed genuinely eager to act on his offer to organize a celebratory banquet in Hugo's honor. It turned out that for this particular event, Hugo did have some people to invite after all. Seven people.

Robert and Jackson arrived first. Hugo had not seen either since returning from Dallas, having told Jackson he came back with a slight case of bronchitis. The specifics were a lie, but not the general proposition of illness.

He had barely said words of greeting to Robert and Jackson when Melinda, the airline ticket agent, came in with former marine Matt Columbia, the Fish and Wildlife agent, just back from South America.

Matt said, "Are you letting your hair grow back?"

Hugo only smiled and said, "Just have a good time, Matt." He had not shaved since arriving back in Washington three nights ago.

With Melinda, there was a brief exchange of kisses on the cheek. "You look so different — but so great," she said. At first Hugo didn't get it, but then he realized Melinda had not seen him in his former-marine look.

And here came Emily, rather smartly dressed — for Emily. She had on a double-breasted worsted-wool gray blazer with large gold buttons and a below-the-knee desert-brown skirt made of what appeared to be a soft cotton, possibly with a bit of polyester. Melinda was in a single-piece worsted-wool dress that had crisp white linen cuffed long sleeves and a matching collar.

"What are you up to?" Emily asked Hugo in the best stage whisper she could manage.

"All in good time," Hugo said.

"That's what I'm afraid of," she replied.

The last guests to arrive were the two most important. Judge McIllhenny of the D.C. Superior Court and Dalton T. Andrews. They walked in within a few minutes of each other. In both cases, Hugo had had to talk fast to secretaries just to get his invitation in to the important man. He'd had scant hopes of either attending, but he felt each should know he had been invited. He had thought also of inviting Art Buchwald and Mark Russell but decided neither would come and both would understand later why they hadn't been asked.

"Wouldn't have missed it," said the judge, wearing a charcoal three-button suit with a white shirt and a large blue-and-white-striped bow tie. This street outfit, to Hugo's observation, was as much a social uniform for the judge as his robe was at work. "They're still talking about you, Mr. Marder, around the courthouse."

"I can't stay the whole evening," said Mr. Andrews. "I hope a short presence and a few quick words are permissible." He was dressed in a navy hopsack suit Hugo had sold him six years ago, plus his secretary of defense cuff links with an ecru button-down broadcloth shirt. His tie was a perfect yellow-dotted dark green silk. Hugo had taught him well.

Hugo picked up a fresh glass of champagne. It was gone in a matter of a few breaths and seconds. It was as if he had sniffed the cold bubbly through his nose. Swoosh! The glass was immediately refilled, and he emptied it again. Swoosh!

Judge McIllhenny and Mr. Andrews, at You Johnny's suggestion, sat down at the table on either side of Hugo after being introduced around. The others, who were told to sit wherever they liked, seemed most impressed at being in the company of the secretary and the judge. Emily in particular, of course. Hugo didn't even want to consider what she might be thinking.

Hugo's seat between these two men made him feel more influential than he ever had. Because he knew that feeling was temporary, he wanted to make the most of it. It was accompanied, in a relentless counterpoint, by a sense of dirtiness, fraudulence — disgust — about himself. This feeling, he assumed, would be permanent.

You Johnny was still standing. He clinked his glass with a knife. Everyone fell silent.

"Mr. Secretary, Your Honor, ladies and gentlemen. Welcome to the most hallowed moment we have ever had here at our simple, most unworthy restaurant."

Looking at the secretary, he said, "No one of your stature and meaning has ever come through our doors and up these steps, Mr. Secretary. When Mr. Marder's work colleagues informed me of your regularity as his customer, I was so pleased. When I was

informed that you were coming here tonight, I was brought to a state of enormous
elation. Thank you for helping us honor a
man who qualifies to be called, by one and
by all, a true American hero."

You Johnny now had a glass of something
orange in his right hand. He moved his
adoring gaze to Hugo.

"Hugo Marder, we salute and revere you
as the ultimate hero. You were a hero for
your country on the battlefield, and then
you were a hero again for your country in
the hallowed halls of our system of justice. I
toast you, sir, and ask that all here join me."

Everyone raised a glass. Hugo looked at
Melinda, who was sitting directly across the
table. She was teary. Please don't cry — not
yet, at least. What was that song from that
Madonna movie? "Don't cry for me, Argen-
tina"? Hugo could stand and belt out,
"Don't cry for me, dear Melinda!" What a
crazy thought!

Mr. Andrews rose with a glass that appeared to be filled with water. "I would at-
tach a simple 'amen' to those good words. I
am pleased to be present here tonight and
to second that toast."

After Mr. Andrews sat, Judge McIllhenny
stood and said, "I second that 'amen'— and
forthwith and therefore, by the power vested

in me, order everyone else to do the same."

There were laughs and cries of "hear-hear!" and clinks of glasses. Hugo half stood and leaned to exchange glass hits with every guest. He sat back down and emptied his glass. Swoosh!

"Speech, sir?" You Johnny called out to Hugo.

Jackson Dyer said, "Yes, yes, let's hear from Hugo."

"Later," Hugo said, and waved away the suggestion.

The waiters swept the table of the appetizers and quickly replaced them with larger platters of entrées — strips of beef and chicken and pork and fish cooked a variety of ways, mixed in with a variety of vegetables and sauces and spices. You Johnny or one of the waiters carefully identified and described each dish. There were names such as King Pad Ped, Gaeng Gai, Kapow Delight, Panang Perfect, Goong Pad Pak, and Hugo's favorite title, Kanom Jeen Num Prik. There were also bowls of fried brown and boiled white rice and many kinds of noodles.

"A dinner fit for a Thai king — and for an American hero," said You Johnny as they began passing the platters among them, family-style. Hugo wasn't hungry, but, out of courtesy and a need for something to go with the champagne, he filled his plate to overflowing and used his fork — with an imprint of an elephant in the handle — to move the food around a bit.

Mostly, he went to work on another glass of champagne — not quite a swoosh! this time — and tried to go over what he would say once the time came.

And he excused himself to go to the bathroom. He wasn't sick. He simply wanted to get away for a few minutes. Both Mr. Andrews and Judge McIllhenny were more than occupied with questions from the others. He recalled seeing a MEN sign on a door at the bottom of the stairs, and he headed for it.

"Hugo." It was a familiar female voice. It was Emily coming down the stairs behind him. He stopped. Once she caught up, he said, "No, I don't need to be serviced now, if that's what you have in mind. But thanks."

That got her. She seemed to jump away, clearly taken aback by his coarseness.

But she recovered instantly and resumed her usual frowning posture with Hugo. "What's this about? That's all I want to know."

"You'll know soon," Hugo said.

"Don't do anything stupid, that's all I

ask," Emily said as she walked away, shaking her head like the disappointed mother of a wayward — or profoundly stupid — child.

In the men's room, Hugo didn't do much more than run his hand over the top of his head, which felt like a thin doormat made of soft new grass. He also used the mirror to admire the special ensemble he had worn for this special evening. The suit, one of the best in his wardrobe, was a three-button navy blue pure wool in an intricate basket weave. Suits like this were the very top of the Nash Brothers line and, even with his discount, it had cost more than $1,000. The pastel blue straight-collar broadcloth dress shirt seemed made for the Statue of Liberty cuff links he was wearing. His tie was a $95 silk Jim Thompson burgundy with small white elephants, in honor of the Thai connection.

While still at the mirror, Hugo, on nervous reflex, began a silent, mouthed rehearsal of the words he intended to speak later.

He heard the door open. There behind him was You Johnny. "I'm so sorry, Mr. Marder," he said. "But Secretary Andrews said he must leave in a very few minutes."

Hugo would now try to speak his words out loud.

■ ■ ■ ■

Hugo did not sit back down. He simply moved to his place at the table and started talking.

"This is indeed a banquet to remember, and I will always be grateful to you for having provided it, You Johnny. I also appreciate all of you coming here this evening on such short notice."

There. Yes, that was the easy part. But at least he had begun.

Everyone — except Emily — was looking at him with admiration and esteem pouring from their eyes. Tears were still in Melinda's, but at least they weren't pouring. Robert's demeanor was that of pride, a friend who was happy for a friend. And he was the only one here besides Emily who knew the truth.

That was going to change — right now.

"You are here, I regret to say, under very false pretenses. This is not an event for celebration but for revelation," Hugo said, remembering the words he had written and memorized. "Tomorrow I plan to contact a *Washington Herald* reporter named Lisa Winfield. I doubt if any of you remember, but she was the one who wrote the story about me that included not only what happened at the courthouse but also what she was told about my background."

Hugo, intent on his message, now avoided eye contact with anyone. He moved his right hand up to the lapel on his suit coat.

"As you may have noticed, the Silver Star pin, the tiny badge of honor and valor, is not there. It never will be again. The reason is that the pin and the medal it stands for do not belong to me. They were won by a man named Ronald Derby Cunningham. I have never been to Vietnam. I was not a U.S. Marine. I was not in the service at all. My only connection to the marines was a boyhood urge to be one, an urge I later ignored when the opportunity — the responsibility — presented itself to me. I reinvented myself as a former marine. I have stolen the honors of others, and I have stolen your esteem under the falsest of false pretenses.

"That is what I will tell the *Washington Herald* reporter. But my confession to all of you is more critical than any general public one. That's why I wanted you to know directly from me before you read it in the newspaper."

He stopped talking.

He looked at each of the silent faces

around the table. None showed any reaction. Not Melinda's. Not even Mr. Andrews's, whose response Hugo dreaded the
most, and Judge McIllhenny's. Emily was
shaking her head in obvious disbelief and
annoyance with the confirmed stupidity of
this man to whom she was once married.
The others seemed paralyzed. Had they not
heard what Hugo said? Did they not believe
him?

Hey, Matt, what's wrong? Aren't you going to *Move out!* against me?

Hugo said it again. "This is not a joke. I
have been wearing a Silver Star pin, and I
have been claiming the honor that goes with
it, but neither is mine. Not the Silver Star,
not the honor. I am an impostor. I bought a
whole medal set — the case, the medal
itself, plus the ribbon and the lapel pin —
in an eBay auction on the Internet for
eighty-five dollars. Using information from
books, video and audiotapes, and the Internet, I reinvented myself as a former marine.
The shaved head, the trim body, the altered
walk, the concocted service record — all of
it was to make you and everyone else believe
I was an authentic marine, an authentic
hero. Nothing could be further from the
truth."

That brought Matt to life. "So we're talking an Admiral Boorda kind of thing here, is that it?" he blurted.

"That's right — only worse. He was a real naval officer who only added a small enhancement to a medal he had legitimately earned —"

"Yes, that is certainly true. *This* is so, so much worse than anything Mike Boorda did." It was Mr. Andrews. He stood, buttoned his blue hopsack coat, pulled his shoulders back, and said, "There are no words to adequately express my disappointment with you, Hugo. I am sorry to say, a sad feeling of utter and complete contempt comes with my disappointment."

Mr. Andrews gave a dramatic but dignified nod in the direction of You Johnny and moved toward the door.

"Mr. Andrews, please," said Judge McIllhenny, who was standing. "I would ask that you stay a few more moments. I know you have another engagement —"

"I am leaving out of disgust, Judge," said Mr. Andrews. "It has nothing to do with prior engagements."

"Very well. Then please let's not forget, sir, that we came here tonight to celebrate not what Mr. Marder did or didn't do in Vietnam but what he did in my courtroom. That, sir, I can assure you was an act that deserves our praise."

Mr. Andrews, it was clear, was not a man used to being stopped on his way out of any place or event — or conclusion. But he did move a step back toward the table, obviously only a temporary pause out of respect for the judge.

Judge McIllhenny continued his brief. "One might also suggest, sir, that if heroism is what is before us now, then maybe we should ask Mr. Marder why he has chosen to voluntarily expose himself publicly as a fraudulent war hero. May I pose that question to you, Mr. Marder?"

Hugo had not come prepared to be questioned. He had assumed his announcement would promptly clear the room and his life of all these people — forever.

But he told of meeting Phil Cacivio in Dallas, a man who wore a Navy Cross lapel pin and claimed to have been a marine officer in Vietnam.

"I suspected that he, like me, was a fraud. Then, when I found out he was genuine, I hated myself for suspecting such a thing of another man — a real hero. It was sick. I was sick. I got even sicker after reading about a young marine lieutenant from Texas and several other marines who were just killed in Iraq."

Hugo dropped his head and murmured, "That's when I realized I had to end this. I was dishonoring real marines like Ron Cunningham and the man in Dallas and all others like them." He expected everyone to spit on him and be gone.

Mr. Andrews stayed put. Judge McIllhenny crossed his arms across his chest judicially and moved his gaze to the others.

Jackson Dyer's face was crimson. With rage? Embarrassment? Probably a little of both — no, a *lot* of both. Hugo, after raising his eyes to look around, said to Jackson, "You have my resignation, Jackson. I know that Nash Brothers cannot have an associate who has done such things. Integrity and honesty are musts. Please pass on my apologies to my colleagues here and in Dallas and to headquarters in New York. There is nothing I would ever do intentionally to hurt the reputation of the company I love. I hope you know that. I apologize in advance for the bad publicity this might bring to Nash Brothers. I am so, so sorry."

Jackson looked away.

Melinda, her eyes now clear of tears, stared at Hugo. He couldn't tell if it was with hate or loathing or simple confusion.

Robert, probably the most naturally articulate person in the room, remained seated but began speaking to Hugo.

"Now, let's not lose our heads here, Sir Hugo. You may not have earned that medal specifically, but as the judge said, you certainly demonstrated at the courthouse that you are a brave man. As I have said to you before, heroism is a matter of opportunity, not of the soul. You have a splendid soul, my friend."

"Now I really must go," said Mr. Andrews.

Robert said to him, "I would ask that you contemplate joining all of us — *all* of us at this table — in a vow of silence about what we have heard from Hugo tonight. I would urge you to join us in imploring Hugo to forgo that call tomorrow to *The Washington Herald.* Yes, he should not have worn another man's medal, and yes, he should not have posed as a former member of America's most distinguished military force. But I would respectfully suggest: Does not what he did in Judge McIllhenny's courtroom and, even here tonight, coming forward in an act of conscience, clearly constitute heroic acts in and of themselves?"

Robert picked up his glass. "I say let's have another glass of champagne and let the celebration of Hugo Marder continue."

"Yes, yes," Melinda said. Hugo saw that she was about to cry again.

"No way!" It was Matt. Hugo was surprised it had taken him this long to really speak up. "He made fools of all of us. He dishonored the Corps. He deserves to fry in the *Herald* — and in hell." He turned to Melinda. "Let's get the fuck out of here."

Hugo listened for a gasp at Matt's use of the F-word in such company. There was none.

Melinda spoke quietly but with feeling to Matt: "But also, what about what Hugo did for you and me and everyone right here in this restaurant the other night? You said yourself that his coolness saved lives."

Matt was on his feet. "It doesn't erase his lies." He moved toward the door. Melinda, following, said to Hugo, "Matt's right, I guess. I respected you because I thought you were a Silver Star, like my dad. Matt's right, Matt's right — I guess."

"Not only are you worse than Boorda, you're worse than Nixon," said Matt.

He and Melinda became the first to depart the Chiang Mai Room.

Nixon? thought Hugo. I have ruined myself just like Nixon? Wearing another man's Silver Star and lying about being a former marine were the same as engineering the Watergate cover-up?

Judge McIllhenny said, "There goes our

chance at a unanimous jury verdict. What about you, Mr. Secretary? If we can prevail on Hugo not to reveal his story beyond this room, will you also keep it to yourself?"

Mr. Andrews blinked a couple of times, again raised his shoulders, and said, "It is something I must sleep on. I do have one question for Hugo. What did you do with the Silver Star medal . . . the pin and so forth?"

"I have returned them to their proper place," Hugo said.

"Good. And good evening."

Mr. Andrews took his leave.

In less than a minute, so did the judge. His last words were: "The decision about the *Herald* is yours, Mr. Marder. None of us can do any more."

"Thank you," said Hugo.

Now there were only Robert and Jackson and Emily.

She was still shaking her head — in disbelief? Disgust? Hugo had barely looked at her, but now he wondered if she had been showing her disapproval this way throughout.

"You are an asshole idiot if you spill your guts to the press," said Emily. "You finally made something of yourself, for chrissake. Don't throw it away."

And it was goodbye one more time to Emily, a woman who clearly believed making something phony of yourself was just terrific.

Once she was gone, it was obvious Jackson wished he had left earlier. He seemed most uncomfortable with just Robert and Hugo. You Johnny was there, too, but he didn't count.

"Are you in agreement with Judge McIllhenny's arrangement?" Robert began, clearly confirming Jackson's fears.

"Conspiracy, you mean," said Jackson. The redness was gone from his face but not the distress.

Robert and Jackson were talking as if Hugo were not sitting across the table from them.

"Call it what you wish," Robert said. "The question is: Are you willing to — to use the judge's word — forgo spreading the story of Hugo's sins, which, in your case, means to headquarters in New York?"

"He's already resigned. You heard him."

"You can simply refuse to accept the resignation."

That was it. Jackson shoved himself and his chair away from the table. " 'Simply' is a word that does not apply to any of this.

"You were the best suits man I ever knew,"

he said to Hugo at the door. "I'm sorry it had to end this way."

Robert said, "So, I read from that response, Jackson, that the answer to my inquiry is no. No, you will not protect Hugo —"

"Like Secretary Andrews, I have to sleep on it."

Robert Masefield gave Hugo a long, firm hug as they said their farewells. The unspoken probability was that the farewells were forever. They had barely begun developing personal ties that might have continued without the store relationship. But they weren't quite there yet.

"You had dodged all of the bullets, Hugo, you had pulled it off," said Robert. "Nobody would have ever known. You could have gone to Dallas . . ."

Hugo was shaking his head. Robert stopped talking. But only for a few seconds. Then he said, "Mr. Andrews and Jackson are willing to sleep on their next move. I implore, plead, and beg of you to do the same about yours. Will you join our conspiracy — at least for another twenty-four hours or so?"

"I don't know," Hugo said. "I honestly don't know."

"In the Cypriot diplomatic corps, we

would take such an answer to our bosom and proclaim it as progress."

And then there was only You Johnny.

You Johnny's shirt and tie and suit seemed as fresh as when the evening began. So did his straight, thin well-cut black hair and his soft demeanor.

Hugo moved to leave, but, with his right hand, You Johnny motioned for him to stay.

"Why did you really do this, Mr. Marder?" he asked.

"I had no choice, Mr. . . . please, tell me your last name so that I may speak to you properly."

"It's really not that complicated. I will say it slowly, sir, and you may repeat after me. First part, 'Boony.' "

" 'Boony.' That's easy."

" 'Amalik.' Boony-amalik."

" 'Amalik.' Boonyamalik."

" 'Choo-ka-la.' Boony-amal-ik-choo-ka-la."

"Boony-amal-ik-choo-ka-la. Boonyama-likchookala. Mr. Boonyamalikchookala. Yes, that's much better."

You Johnny took a sip of his orange drink. Hugo took one of champagne. A full glass remained in front of him. He hadn't had any more to drink since returning from the men's room. He had drunk four, maybe five glasses before. He felt not a trace of any of it now. In fact, he wasn't sure if he had ever been more sober in his life. Could it be that confession of a mortal sin worked well as a sobering countermeasure to the effects of alcohol?

"I would like to agree with one statement that was made about what you did here a few moments ago, Mr. Marder," said You Johnny. "Whatever you may think of yourself and speak of yourself, sir, you are truly a brave man."

"I am a fraud —"

You Johnny held up his left hand for silence. "Even if you don't go to the press yourself, just by saying what you said here, you have cocked a weapon that could lead you down a course toward bringing ruin to yourself. I listened to what was said. You could be sacrificing your position as a treasured man of clothes, your relationship with your working colleagues, your personal situation with friends, your public reputation — your basic existence. No one will give you a medal or a certificate, but you have acted well. You must understand and treasure that about yourself, Mr. Marder."

It was a thought. Hugo vowed to someday

consider it. But not now, not at this moment.

"Allow me to toast you again," said You Johnny.

Hugo reached across, and once more they touched glasses and took long sips.

"Thank you, sir," Hugo said. "You are a good and honorable man."

A large smiled came to You Johnny's tranquil Thai face. "Oh, Mr. Marder, allow me to share with you a fact that may change that exalted opinion of me." He gently swept his right hand through the air, as if to cover the room and the restaurant. "I never worked for Mr. Jim Thompson. I never ever laid either of my eyes upon him, in fact, except fleetingly one hot July afternoon on the street in front of the Oriental Hotel in Bangkok. I invented the relationship in order to enhance the story behind this restaurant."

Hugo was stunned. And it must have showed.

You Johnny said, "Did you think you were the only one who wished to be something he was not? You are part of a universal movement within the human spirit, Mr. Marder."

"You made up the You Johnny thing, too?"

"I did, sir. I am quite proud of that bit of

creativity, if I may be so boastful."

Hugo said nothing. They sat in silence for several seconds.

Then Mr. Boonyamalikchookala, alias You Johnny, said, "So when I say that what you did tonight was heroic, I know of what I speak, sir. I know it because I know that I could not have done it. It is conceivable that I, if thrust into such a situation and despite my diminutive size, could act with honor and bravery on the battlefield or even, sir, the way you did at the courthouse. Those would be acts of spontaneous heroism. But what you did tonight was premeditated."

Hugo had nothing more to say.

"Here now, Mr. Marder," You Johnny said after a few more seconds of silence. He again reached his glass toward Hugo, who again met it with his.

"What is that orange stuff in there, by the way?" Hugo asked.

Mr. Boonyamalikchookala leaned across the table as if about to reveal a valuable and dangerous secret. "Can I trust you not to report me to the dedicated authorities of the United States Department of the Interior?" he said in an exaggerated whisper.

"You can, sir."

He held his glass before him. "This, Mr. Marder, is ice-cold bear claw soup, flavored and colored by a dash of freshly squeezed orange juice. It is a choice warm-weather drink served only in the most supreme of the dining and drinking clubs of Asia."

From her voice on the phone, Hugo had imagined Lisa Winfield to be middle-aged and large.

Wrong. She was a thin — skinny, really — woman in her early thirties with close-cropped black hair and tiny features. Only her voice and manner were substantial.

On the phone, she had listened to Hugo explain who he was and ask to see her on an urgent matter.

" 'Urgent' meaning what, exactly, Mr. Marder?" she said.

"I have a confession to make."

She immediately agreed to meet him for lunch at Simenon's, Hugo's neighborhood French place, just up the street from the House on the Klong.

And now, brief introductory small talk done, notepad and pen at the ready, she said, "You're on, Mr. Marder."

As with his speech last night, Hugo had, in the three hours between the call and the rendezvous, rehearsed as best he could.

"To put it bluntly, I am a fraud," he began, and watched as Lisa Winfield wrote that in her notebook, which had REPORTER NOTEBOOK printed in large type across its cardboard cover.

Seldom looking up at him, she continued to write as he told the story about the Silver Star pin acquisition and how it had led to his falsifying a past life as a U.S. Marine hero and a current one as a former marine. Many of the specific words and phrases came directly from his House on the Klong confession.

Toward the end of his sorry saga, he noticed that Lisa Winfield's writing gradually began to slow down. Finally, she stopped moving the pen across pages.

He had been describing how he had accepted a free chicken gyro sandwich.

She wasn't taking any of it down anymore, though her eyes remained on the notebook. She seemed to have either lost track of what he was saying or gone on thinking about something else.

"What's wrong, Ms. Winfield?" he asked.

She looked up at him, drew in a deep breath, released it, and then leaned toward him. There were only a few people in the restaurant, which was decorated with framed photos of Simenon smoking a pipe, book jackets of Simenon novels, posters from movies made from those novels, plus empty calvados bottles of various sizes and origins. Hugo knew all about calvados, Simenon's favorite drink, from an earlier evening here.

Lisa Winfield whispered, "I am going to take the position that everything you have just told me was off the record."

Hugo was startled — and then, after a second's further thought, totally confused. "What does that mean?" he asked.

"It means there will be no story in the *Herald.* I cannot use information that is given to me off the record, not even if I attribute it to well-camouflaged sources."

Hugo still didn't get it. "The whole point of this was for you to do a story in the paper. I want to clear the air so I can get on with my life."

She shook her head. And closed her notebook. "My original story should stand," she said, still whispering. "It was about your heroism at the courthouse. There was nothing about it that was fraudulent. You acted heroically — end of story."

"But you also wrote about my Silver Star and service in the Marine Corps in Vietnam —"

She batted that away with her hand. "There would have been a story about what you did at the courthouse even without that.

Go about your life, Mr. Marder. Put this behind you."

Hugo was caught in a mix of emotions. What in the hell is going on with this woman? he thought.

So he said to her, "Something here does not make sense, Ms. Winfield."

"Mr. Marder, this is about my career as a journalist." Her voice was barely audible. "I write up what you just told me, and that story could very well become my ticket to oblivion."

Hugo tried to understand how that could be. She must have seen from his face that he was still a long way from following.

"Mr. Marder, let me be as honest and open — and off the record — with you as you have been with me." Hugo was tempted to say he had never asked that anything be off the record, but he didn't.

She continued, "First, let me tell you that my original story about you received wide and lavish praise from my editors and *Herald* readers. There is a strong chance that it may be entered in several journalism contests for excellence in breaking-news coverage. Second, if my editors were to read your confession, they would immediately ask me if I checked out your Silver Star, Vietnam, marine claims before I wrote the original story. I would have to say, 'No, I didn't.' They would ask me, 'Why not?' I would say I was under deadline pressure. They would say that doesn't wash, because military records like this are available within minutes from various public sources. Third, I am in line to be transferred from the metro desk to the national desk, a move that most likely would never happen if I did this new story about you. On the contrary, in the current post–Jayson Blair atmosphere, I might even be fired. I trust you now can understand what I am saying. A story about what you have just told me could end up being the instrument of my own destruction. I don't know if it's possible to put it any plainer than that."

Hugo, who had been matching her lean across the table, sat back as if pushed.

She was still talking. "This can only work for both of us, of course, if we make a mutual-destruction pact. You must agree never to repeat your confession to any other newsperson or organization. We both, here and now, over our respective glasses of red wine that I will put on my *Washington Herald* expense account, take a kind of Deep Throat blood oath of silence that goes with us to our respective graves."

He made the snap decision not to tell her

about his House on the Klong confession. There were already several people out there who knew the truth. But mutual-destruction pacts mean . . . well, mutual risk?

"Do we have a deal, Mr. Marder?" Lisa Winfield asked, holding up her wineglass.

Hugo grabbed his glass and, after a few seconds' delay, reached across and banged it against hers.

# Seven Months Later

Hugo's graying dark blond hair is almost back to its old thinness on top and its fullness around the edges and sideburns.

He has spoken the F-word out loud within the hearing of another person only once in the seven months. That was to Emily, when she telephoned to confirm that the lack of a story in the *Herald* meant he had decided against a dramatic public confession. Then she asked, one more time, about remarrying.

Hugo is once again at work on L Street in suits/sport coats, having been invited by Jackson, who, after "sleeping on it" for nine weeks, decided to go along with Robert's suggested conspiracy of silence. Jackson first wanted confirmation that no one else was talking and that no story would appear in the *Herald.*

At Jackson's suggestion, Hugo wears the red and white pin of the District of Columbia Medal of Honor in his coat lapel at work. Hugo's first reaction had been negative, but that went away, particularly after it led to some solid sales. He really had earned *that* medal.

On the evening of his return to the store, Hugo treated Robert to dinner at a nearby upscale restaurant called the Cloakroom, a dark-paneled steak house that featured eight different kinds of martinis and large oil paintings of congressional leaders, past and present. Hugo has since been to Robert's home four times for dinner, and he has entertained Robert and his family at Nineteenth Street on five occasions.

Making friends at the store and elsewhere is a transformation attribute that has stayed with him. He attends a Wednesday-evening social hour for singles at a nearby church, and he has become a regular volunteer at a social outreach center for the homeless over on Eighteenth Street.

There has been only one incident arising from the overlap of his old and new lives. That came on a recent Sunday morning, when he prepared an elaborate first-date brunch for a woman he had met at church. She is June Chrisman, a self-described "happy divorcée from a quick, stupid marriage," an attractive blonde with a great laugh and figure and a job as an economic statistician at the Federal Reserve.

For an extra dish, Hugo dug out that recipe of shit on a shingle he had printed off the Internet. The dish came out fine, and he put the piping-hot creamed beef and toast on the kitchen counter along with orange juice, scrambled eggs, bagels, and other breakfast treats.

"Help yourself to the S.O.S.," Hugo said without thinking to June.

"S.O.S.? What does that stand for?"

Hugo was not about to say shit-on-a-shingle on a first date. In a flash of *Move out!* creativity, he said, "Sally's Own Soup."

"Who was Sally?" asked June.

"My mother," said Hugo, not telling a lie.

But the real high point came when Hugo, on impulse, pulled out an old sketchbook and, with a soft lead pencil, did an instant portrait of June. She seemed most impressed.

There has been nothing but silence about Hugo's brief fraudulent life as a marine hero. There has been no news story by Lisa Winfield, and there have been no alarms about or confrontations with anyone who was at the House on the Klong confessional.

Hugo knows this does not mean it's over. On any given day, Lisa Winfield could have an ambitious change of heart, or one of the banquet-goers could decide to break the silence. Matt is still out there. He definitely did not agree to remain silent. Neither, technically, did Melinda, although Hugo has trouble imagining her publicizing his dishonors. She still wanted him to be a Silver Star.

There is also a possibility that Phil Cacivio might, through some marine happenstance, stumble across the fact that Hugo, the man who didn't come to Dallas after all, was a phony marine and Silver Star. That could get trickier if the company rumor mill about P. J. Rodriguez turns out to be correct. The word is that Jackson may soon be on his way to managing the mother store in New York and that P.J. will be promoted to replace him in Washington. If that happens, it's always possible that Phil Cacivio could follow her again. The rumor mill has been silent about that. No matter what Phil problems there might be, the upside to P.J.'s coming to L Street would be having such a beautiful woman to look at every day. Another Nash Brothers perk.

Whatever, there is no doubt that a Crucible of risks continues for Hugo.

Among the potential threats is the one of his own conscience. On any given day, a new storm of guilt could slam him into making a second effort at coming publicly clean. Although, as time passes, the likelihood of that happening is diminishing.

Hugo remains on the South Beach diet and the Semper Fit exercises, and the old pre-marine bounce has not returned to his step. He still walks and carries himself very much like a marine and, in his own mind at least, continues to live the transformation.

Only the lies, the phony parts, are gone.

He's even recently begun to have occasional flashes of believing he really once was a U.S. Marine.

# ACKNOWLEDGMENTS

I wish to thank several friends, most of them former marines, for their help. Jim Dickenson and Richard Anderson read an early manuscript and made good suggestions. Dickenson also provided an audiotape of the Smithsonian session that he moderated. Mark Russell and Art Buchwald granted permission to use their famous names and words from that same discussion. Frank Reilly told me what I needed to know about the men's clothing business. Bill Crowe suggested there was a relevant Edmund Gwenn movie I should see. John Redgate gave me a copy of *Marine Rifleman,* the superb book by Wesley L. Fox. Bob Loomis, my editor at Random House, did his usual extraordinary job of turning a manuscript into something publishable.

I also want to express my appreciation for the bits and pieces of assistance I received from various marine writings, tapes, and movies that I mention by name throughout the book.

LEHRER, JAMES C., 071278/0302

# ABOUT THE AUTHOR

**Jim Lehrer** served as a Marine Corps infantry officer in the 1950s. His father and brother were also marines. This is his sixteenth novel. He's also the author of two memoirs and three plays, and is the executive editor and anchor of *The NewsHour with Jim Lehrer* on PBS. He lives in Washington, D.C., with his novelist wife, Kate. They have three daughters.

The employees of Thorndike Press hope you have enjoyed this Large Print book. All our Thorndike and Wheeler Large Print titles are designed for easy reading, and all our books are made to last. Other Thorndike Press Large Print books are available at your library, through selected bookstores, or directly from us.

For information about titles, please call:
(800) 223-1244

or visit our Web site at:
www.gale.com/thorndike
www.gale.com/wheeler

To share your comments, please write:
Publisher
Thorndike Press
295 Kennedy Memorial Drive
Waterville, ME 04901